His arms closed around her powerfully

"Kiss me, Thorn," she said, without the slightest tremor.

"Kiss you?" he muttered, as though he wanted something very different, but as Sue sighed, he lowered his head and cut off her breath.

He slid his hands up and down her back, molding her to him, causing an ardent sexuality to flower within her. She was exploring his mouth as he was exploring hers, her small hands trying to get to the skin beneath his shirt. She couldn't pretend. She was crazy for him.

Thorn lifted her lightly as though she were a feather, seeing the high flush on her cheekbones, her features made more beautiful by intensity.

"Open your eyes, Susan, and I'll stop."

"I don't want to." Her voice was small, rather husky, very far away.

"You're a child. I must protect you. Even from me."

Books by Margaret Way

HARLEQUIN ROMANCES

2203—THE AWAKENING FLAME
2258—WAKE THE SLEEPING TIGER
2265—THE WINDS OF HEAVEN
2276—WHITE MAGNOLIA
2291—VALLEY OF THE MOON
2328—BLUE LOTUS
2346—THE BUTTERFLY AND THE BARON
2357—THE GOLDEN PUMA
2387—LORD OF THE HIGH VALLEY
2400—FLAMINGO PARK
2429—TEMPLE OF FIRE
2435—SHADOW DANCE
2448—A SEASON FOR CHANGE
2454—THE McIVOR AFFAIR
2476—NORTH OF CAPRICORN
2490—HOME TO MORNING STAR
2537—SPELLBOUND
2556—HUNTER'S MOON
2591—THE GIRL AT COBALT CREEK

HARLEQUIN PRESENTS

 78—A MAN LIKE DAINTREE
 82—COPPER MOON
 94—BAUHINIA JUNCTION
102—THE RAINBOW BIRD
134—STORM FLOWER
154—RED CLIFFS OF MALPARA
270—RING OF FIRE
549—BROKEN RHAPSODY

These books may be available at your local bookseller.

For a free catalog listing all titles currently available, send your name and address to:

Harlequin Reader Service
2504 West Southern Avenue, Tempe, AZ 85282
Canadian address: Stratford, Ontario N5A 6W2

The Girl at Cobalt Creek

Margaret Way

Harlequin Books

TORONTO • NEW YORK • LONDON
AMSTERDAM • PARIS • SYDNEY • HAMBURG
STOCKHOLM • ATHENS • TOKYO • MILAN

Original hardcover edition published in 1983
by Mills & Boon Limited

ISBN 0-373-02591-2

Harlequin Romance first edition December 1983

CHAPTER ONE

'NOT people again!' her mother wailed; even then with a good deal of style.

'Just for the weekend. About twelve in all. I'll try and keep them out of your way.'

'Really, Sue!' Patricia, her senior by four years, jumped on the band wagon. 'The house simply isn't our own any more! How you ever got this revolting idea of turning our home into a guesthouse and the property into some kind of cheap camping ground, I'll never know!'

She could have been very rude, instead she was brusque. 'Would you prefer to lose it?'

'Well . . .' Patricia flushed under her sister's direct, green-eyed gaze, 'why not? What's so sacred about an old cattle run?'

'*Patricia!*' The hollow, shocked tone demanded an instant apology.

They're imbeciles, both of them, Susan lamented.

'Oh, I'm sorry, Mummy!' Patricia, as always, did exactly what her mother required. Perched on the arm of her mother's chair, she was now awash with remorse.

'Even so, Patricia.'

'We can't pretend it's the old days, Mummy.'

'I know that better than you,' Julia coldly reproved her favourite daughter. 'However, you have the great good fortune to be living in one of the most beautiful historic homesteads in the country.'

'And yet, in its way, it's a burden,' sighed Susan.

'Because it needs so much money!' Julia bit her thin, finely cut lips. 'It needs men, not three helpless, inexperienced women.'

'I'm not helpless, you know!' Susan exclaimed. In fact she was bidding fair to become like Grandmother Alice Drummond who had run Cobalt Downs when the men were away at war.

'Helpless or not, you're a mere girl!' Julia said scornfully. 'We seem to be getting by at the moment, but ultimately we'll go under. Your dear father worked so hard it finally killed him. No one can tell me differently. Not ever. Cobalt Downs killed my husband and left me a widow—alone and afraid.'

'You have me, Mummy!' Patricia said without hesitation, but Susan felt a surge of uncontrollable grief. She whirled away from her mother and sister and went to stand at the huge picture window that looked out over the beautiful, tree-studded valley. It was a broad canvas that she knew well— emerald green downs, cobalt blue hills, a magnificent lagoon that was in itself a fantasy, a splendid mirror-smooth sheet of water ringed by great clusters of the white arum lily that flowered continuously and the home of the black swans and the countless ducks that revelled in its serene loveliness. She badly wanted to cry, but she could no more afford the luxury than she could judge her mother and sister too harshly. They were soft people, the protected ones, too easily hurt by the reversal in the family fortunes.

'You love it so much, don't you, Susan?' her mother asked kindly.

'Love it?' Susan answered almost violently. 'Oh, yes, I *love* it. I'd like to forget it sometimes too, but I can't. There have been Drummonds here for more than a hundred and fifty years. That's a long time in our part of the world, but love of the land is nothing new for a Drummond. It goes back many centuries and it goes deep.'

'Oh, Sue, you do have such a sense of theatre!' Patricia burst out, embarrassed. 'How can any girl get all worked up about the few hundred acres that are still left to us?'

'If you don't know, we can't talk about it.'

'No, and it's not possible to forget Daddy left you the controlling interest. *You*, the youngest!'

'But only because he knew I would look after it!' Susan ardently defended her father's decision. 'We all have our home, and Daddy was always very fair.'

'Of course he was.' Julia Drummond patted her elder daughter's slim white hand. 'Daddy always knew best. We were all provided for in different ways.'

'But Susan always came first!' Patricia's lovely face was marred by her jealous pangs.

'So Daddy and Susan were the same kind of people? Aren't *we* the closest friends?'

'Of course we are, Mummy.' Patricia lost her aggrieved pout. 'I just can't help thinking we'd all be a lot better off if we sold out and settled into city life. Neither you nor I are countrywomen at heart, and Peter will never come back.'

'Peter comes back all the time,' Susan said abruptly, missing her brother more than she could ever mention.

'You're so quick-tempered,' Patricia sighed. 'Almost gruff. It's only people like you who persist with this family legend thing. So the Drummonds were once wealthy pastoralists? We're not any more and we never will be again. As Mummy said, no men. Granddad lost three brothers in the war and he only had one child, and that was Daddy.

Even Peter is going to be a doctor, and in case you don't remember, you were the little faithful sister who always egged him on. I know I used to think you were both raving mad. I mean, Daddy was so disappointed.'

Susan shrugged unhappily and returned to her contemplation of the valley. 'When anyone has wanted something as much as Peter wanted to study medicine, they must be given their chance. Besides, Daddy *did* see that Peter just had to be a healer. It all began with the sick or injured animals, then around about ten he started to say he was going to be a doctor.'

'He will be in a few years' time,' Julia said proudly. '*My* Peter, *my* son!' The lovely, slightly faded face came alive with a smile. 'I often think I'd like to be in the city to be beside him—advise him.'

Patricia stole a quick glance at her sister and they both smiled. Much as Julia loved her only son, they were just possibly incompatible, though each managed to triumph over the fact for brief periods at a time. More than a few days and Peter was mad to go back to town, while Julia was almost worn out from her well-meaning nagging.

'*My* Peter!' she said again. 'The most perfect relationship is mother and son. It's an intense, emotional bond.'

'What about daughters, Mummy?' Patricia protested, plunged into an inconsolable jealousy.

'Daughters are different,' Julia answered placidly. 'Absolutely different from having a son. You'll see.'

'I don't see at all.'

'Mummy doesn't mean she doesn't love you just as much!' sensitive Susan attempted to comfort her sister. 'It's just a different love-bond.'

'Oh, I do wish Peter would come home!' Julia wailed.

'He comes back all the time, or as much as he's able,' Susan pointed out quickly. 'Don't ask me to sell out, Mummy. I can't do it.'

'So the land wins every time.' Julia Drummond looked bleak. 'It took your father's life, and now *you're* trying to kill the rest of us off with this odd scheme!'

'It's paying, isn't it?' Susan objected passionately.

'Well, just a pittance.'

'But, Mummy, we eat well and we pay our bills.' Susan felt the deep hurt and the anger, but she kept it under control.

'And is that what you want?' Patricia asked her sister bitterly. 'Just food and shelter?'

'What do *you* want, Paddy?'

'*Paddy!* Charming!' Patricia's porcelain face, a youthful version of her mother's, was clouded with irritation and unhappy anger. 'I've told you not to call me Paddy any more. It's so ridiculous, like a boy!'

'Oh, damn it, is it so important? I've always called you Paddy.'

'And I've never liked it. Surely that's dawned on you.' Patricia's flawless white skin was now a bright pink. 'You've always been the high-spirited tomboy, not me. So you were all things for Daddy? The son he always wanted and never got. I'm a woman, I like womanly things.'

'Then you'd better marry a rich husband,' Susan returned tartly. 'You might even meet one if you'd go out to work. It's only an hour's run into the town.'

'There's no need for Patricia to work,' Julia Drummond protested sharply. 'Would you expect a Drummond to be a little office girl?'

'Why not?' Susan was driven into being blunt.
'When a girl wants to earn money she has to take
what's offering.'

'Even your father disapproved of Patricia's
working,'

'Our lives have changed, Mummy,' Susan said
sadly, trying to swallow her own little flare of
resentment. 'You feel so much for Paddy, yet you
don't seem to care if I work harder than a station
hand.'

'But, my dear, you do by choice, and really,
you're tough! I often disapproved of the way your
father brought you up, but at least it was good
training for the kind of thing we have to do.'

'Why, you don't even wear skirts!' Patricia
added in a wondering voice.

'And why would I wear a skirt when I'm nearly
always on a horse?' Susan contrived to see the
humour, although both her mother and sister were
looking pained. 'The Ashtons will be arriving
tonight and the other people, the Masons and the
Irvings and their party, will be camping along the
creek.'

'How extraordinary that city people should
like roughing it!' Patricia remarked in flat
amazement.

'Maybe they like to taste the sweetness of the
fresh air. We've got a lot going for us here. Guests
can swim and canoe. They can go walking or
riding, play tennis, enjoy the animals or just sit still
and relax and watch the swans. This is beautiful
country. One would have to be blind not to
appreciate the lovely scenery and the unpolluted
air of the valley.'

'Goodness, you sound like a brochure!' Patricia
tinkled.

Susan nodded. 'I've been thinking of getting

some out. But they cost money.'

'And I simply need some new clothes!' Patricia added with a decided air of challenge. 'You might be content to spend your life in a torn shirt and an old pair of jeans, but I like to look nice when I go out.'

'So do I,' Susan grinned. 'Sometimes. Why don't you let Geoff Munro lead you down the garden walk?'

'Geoff is a bore!' Patricia flushed and looked away, her large blue eyes sparkling. 'I want someone with excitement. I want someone who can make me *feel*. Also, he's got to be tall, dark and handsome with plenty of money. I want him to be able to open new doors for me.'

'It will all come for you, darling,' Julia Drummond promised fondly. 'You're so lovely.'

'And I'm not?' Susan asked with a wry twist of her mouth.

'You're . . . unusual, dear.' Julia looked at her younger daughter in mild surprise. 'You will insist on getting so brown you look like a gipsy, but you could be quite attractive if you only took half the trouble your sister does. The first essential is to try and act in a more feminine fashion. I'm touched by the way you work so hard to make a go of things, but by the same token, it's making you bossy. Bossy women I always think are rather *hard*.'

'Would you say I'm hard?' Susan later asked Annie in the kitchen.

'You, hard?' Annie shook her thinning grey head and laughed. 'You, my girl, are a woman with heart.'

'Thanks, Annie,' Susan said simply.

Annie turned a perceptive look upon the girl.

'Sometimes I think your mother and sister are quite cruel.'

'They didn't say anything, Annie,' Susan protested loyally.

'In their nice ladylike fashion, they're continually putting you down,' Annie responded shortly.

'Oh, no, Annie!'

'Oh, yes.' In the persisting unfair situation Annie was goaded into forceful speaking. In the service of the Drummond family for more than forty years Annie never minimised her important position in the household. 'It's a hard life you're leading, love. Hard and lonely.'

'Never!' Susan, who had missed her lunch, bit into an apple.

'There's only me and Spider and your beloved horses to talk to.'

'Then I'm very fortunate in my friends.' Susan gave her beautiful, engaging smile.

'You should be enjoying yourself more,' Annie ignored her, beetling her iron-grey brows. 'And if I can help it, you will. Why should your sister sit around like a bloomin' princess while you work yourself down to the bone?'

'It's natural for me to work, Annie.' Susan finished off the apple and reached for a banana.

'You're so very beautiful too!'

This brought forth a genuine peal of laughter. '*I* am?'

'Yes, you, you little donkey!' Annie said it so angrily, her plump cheeks quivered. 'Not everyone takes your dear mother's view. Of course Patricia is a lovely-looking girl, a porcelain doll. But you're real, vital. Haven't you ever noticed who gets all the glances?'

'Not me, Annie. I know.'

'One half of you knows everything and the other

half knows as little as a new-born baby.' Annie, always composed and cheerful, was positively crotchety.

'It's all getting too much for you, isn't it?' Susan looked into the dear, familiar face with some anxiety. 'You've always been too good for us, Annie. You're nearly sixty and we should be retiring you in splendour. Instead you're working harder than ever. I'll never be able to show all my gratitude.' She bit her lip and hung a small, shapely head covered with glistening dark curls. Was there no way she could make things come right?

But Annie exploded. 'Gratitude!' she burst out positively. 'Goodness, don't I love you too much to talk of gratitude! Why, Susan, I care for you more than anyone else in the whole world. You're the pick of the bunch and I love you all, but when you ask me what's wrong I have to tell you. It's very difficult for me to stand by and watch one small girl turned into a drudge. Holding on to this property, my lamb, is going to be a pitiless task. You're not a man, you can't work with a man's strength. This is a marvellous idea of yours, but we need *staff* as much as spunk!'

'We'll get them once we become better established,' Susan said eagerly. 'All our guests have been the nicest people, and they recommend us to others.'

'All our guests have been so nice they've overlooked a lot of things,' Annie pointed out grimly. 'Of course the valley is beautiful and they'll go a long way to beat my home cooking, but you're getting worn out too quickly. Your mother and sister are what was once known as ladies. That means they scorn work while others less fortunate like you and me are on the go from dawn to dark.'

'Daddy left me in charge.'

'And as much as you love this place, and you know I do too, it may well turn out to be a death sentence. It killed your father, used up his life too quickly. I'm not going to allow the same thing to happen to his daughter.'

'Annie,' Susan made a pathetic little gesture towards this unexpectedly determined woman, 'I'm strong!'

'So am I, love, but overtaxing one's strength can lead to tragedy. Look at you! One apple for lunch.'

'I had breakfast.'

'On the run. I only read the other day where it's bad to stand up.' Annie's blunt, goodhumoured face was serious and stern. 'If you can't persuade your sister to help you, we'll have to hire a girl from the town.'

'That's the point, Annie, we can't afford it now. But soon, I promise you.'

Annie shook her head and clicked her tongue. 'Understand me, lovey—I'd die for you. I've had no other life but your family, no other name but Annie since I came to Cobalt Downs forty odd years ago. I belong here and my loyalties are with you, but I'm not going to stand by and let you kill yourself. You're twenty years of age and you have no fun at all. Come to that, you haven't even got very many clothes, but fortunately you're so slender all the old ones still fit. If we were all working together in harmony we might be able to make a go of this thing, but it's all pretty hopeless without your mamma's and Patricia's co-operation. In fact, another piece of advice. Keep Patricia out of the guests' way. She doesn't trouble to hide her disgust at having paying guests in the house. That's a crime, but apparently she can bear to see her sister who's inches shorter and a good stone lighter run off her feet.'

'*Listen*, Annie,' Susan begged urgently. 'We'll survive. I must bear the brunt of it because I'm the one who's trying to hold on. Drummonds pioneered this valley and I'm not going to let it go without a fight. We have problems, I know. I could never manage without you and Spider, but as soon as they can see there's a future in it, the bank will lend me more money. I'm just waiting to improve the position before I approach them again.'

'You could make yourself very comfortable just selling out,' Annie pointed out bluntly.

'But that I'll never do!' Susan took Annie's plump, ageing face between her two hands and dropped a kiss on her nose. 'You believe me, don't you, Annie?'

'Because of your father, I know.' Annie gave a harsh little laugh that was almost a sob. 'There were times when I wanted to take that dear man to task. There have been Drummonds here since the beginning, but sometimes we have to accept the inevitable.'

'Don't say it, Annie.'

'All right, love,' Annie agreed tenderly. 'I know how you feel.'

'Rich.' Susan went to the open doorway and took a deep breath with infinite pleasure. The air was exquisite, herb and sun scented, and she lifted her slender arms to the encircling blue hills. 'If loving my birthright is a folly, then I'm well content to be a fool.'

To Annie who loved her, the words were beautiful, even noble, yet something to weep over. John Drummond's premature death had been bad, a tragic comment on too hard a life, so it was doubly intolerable to see so young a girl prepared to lay down her life. She thought she was strong, but she wasn't strong at all. Just a mere slip of a girl with far too many responsibilities hung over her head and not another member of the family prepared to shoulder a little of the weight. Peter was a good boy but totally committed to his own career, while Julia and Patricia thought of little but their own comfort.

'Let's face it,' Annie thought sadly, 'we'll be lucky if we survive another year.'

Ten minutes later Susan was in the saddle riding out towards the Quiet Water where she had last seen Spider. Streams of lorikeets were strung out across the sky, piloting her to the large, beautiful stretch of clear water where Spider was working quietly on one of the canoes.

'How's it going?' she asked.

'Nearly done.' Spider busied himself with a few more licks of paint, then laid down his brush. 'Y'know, Susie, I figured this was gunna be a slack time in my life, instead of that there ain't enough hours in the day. Ah well!'

'You've done a very good job, Spider.' Susan sat Persian Princess and looked along the sparkling line of freshly painted canoes. 'I often wonder what I'd do without you.'

'Reckon I'm due for a bit of a spell.' Spider yawned prodigiously and started to unwind himself, tall as a lamp-post, incredibly ungainly, given to long silences and the odd drinking bout but universally described as a 'good, hardy bloke'.

'How about a drink of tea and a bite of something?' Susan smiled at him.

Spider looked back at her and grinned. 'Y'gotta give you credit, Susie. Y'sure know how to keep a man happy, no doubt about that!'

'Here.' Susan passed him the satchel containing a thermos of tea already heavily milked and sugared the way he liked it and a good half of the latest walnut loaf made all the better with thick slabs of butter.

'If anyone were to ask me where you put it all, Spider!'

'I've been skinny as long as I remember. Come to think of it, all us Mathesons are sorta real lean and me Uncle Charlie, y'got no idea how skinny *he* was. Near enough to a skeleton, ya might say. Died when he was ninety-four, ninety-five, some-thin' like that.'

'You're a pretty hard case yourself,' Susan smiled.

'Ya dead right!' Spider settled happily on an upturned canoe. 'Reckon I might last until I'm a coupla hundred. Otherwise you, little lady, are gunna be in trouble.'

'We're making out, Spider.'

'Yeah.' Spider brought out his afternoon tea. 'That sister of yours oughta be ashamed of 'erself, lettin' you handle everything the way you do. An' o'course, ya mum! Well, she ain't used to workin'.'

'I hope you're not going to start again, Spider,' Susan begged him.

'Wouldn't take much for them both to get off their behinds.'

'In another six months, Spider, the worst of it will be over,' she assured him.

'Y'might be married to a millionaire as well.'

'The Ashtons are due late this afternoon,' Susan hastened to head Spider off. 'They're the only ones who want full board. The rest are going to manage for themselves.'

'Any kids?'

'Three. Eight to twelve. They should have a great time.'

'S'pse. I remember the last little bleedin' terrors. Another day in their company and I reckon I'd 'ave drowned 'em!'

'I might have even done something myself,' Susan smiled wryly. 'Anyway, they're not all like that.'

'God love and protect us!' Spider leaned forward to munch at a slab of cake, but the top half broke off and fell on to the ground. 'Bloody hell!' Spider broke into the appropriate blasphemy, reached for the cake and started to clean it up. 'I could do with a bit of a hand, Susie. After all, I'm goin' on sixty. Maybe I could talk ole Bert Cameron into doin' a bit for us. We're so shorthanded both of us are gunna end up dead beat.'

'But surely Bert's nearly eighty?' Susan protested.

'Yeah, but a tough ole buzzard. I might just look 'im up. Reckon he'd keep goin' if we just fed 'im. He was a drover in the old days, worked all the main stock routes. Even now he could walk the legs off a black feller. Only one thing and it's not much. He 'ates women. Reckons they're all bad.'

'Ah well, how's he going to work for one?'

'I'll put it to 'im, this is an emergency. I reckon Dave could be of real assistance with all his experience. He can still stay on a buckin' 'orse.'

'Oh, Spider!' Susan started to laugh, a low melodious sound that was a mixture of tiredness and wry humour. 'Remember the days when there was no shortage of staff at all?'

'Sure I do.' Spider nodded his shaggy head. 'I can never make up my mind about what really finished us, but tryin' to put us back where we was finished your dad.' Spider's gnarled hand began to shake. 'Gawd, how I miss him! My word, I do.

You're your father's daughter, Susie, and I don't know of any greater compliment, but I don't know that tryin' to hold on to this place is good for you You're only one little girl! Hell, I'll work for you until I drop, but can't you see that this ain't no good for you? Ya ain't got no help. Ya family just sit back and take it easy while you work a long, hard day. I've spoken to Annie, and it ain't right.'

'Well, it feels all right to me, Spider,' Susan said. 'I can and will go on.'

'All right, love.' Spider looked up and read the determination in the brilliant green eyes. 'It wouldn't be no disaster if ya could find y'self a fine, strong husband with some ready cash, then ya could start to enjoy y'self again. Ya ten times better-lookin' than ya dainty sister, y'know.'

'Thank goodness someone thinks so,' Susan laughed. 'At least the weather is absolutely beautiful. I hope everyone enjoys themselves.'

'Why shouldn't they?' Spider shoved the thermos back into the satchel and passed it back up to Susan. 'I'll just make another routine inspection, then I'm gunna bloddy well relax.'

Susan too, though she would have been the first one to deny it, was bone-weary, but as she rode on she began to lose herself in the lovely tranquillity of her surroundings. Why was it the valley spoke to her spirit, the hills, the tall gums, the grasslands brightened with wild flowers, the emerald green creek and the large, deep pools? She worshipped the place like an ancient, fighting to keep it when she knew its sale would be of no great moment to the rest of the family. As a child she had been the one who had sat at her grandfather's feet listening to the old stories of the legendary Cobalt Downs. Once they had bred the finest thoroughbred racehorses in the country, run magnificent beef shorthorns that won all the prizes at the Royal Agricultural Show. She could clearly remember the way things had been. Her grandparents had been famous for their open-handed hospitality, the wonderful parties and weekends for friends. Grandpa had been one of the richest men in the State until two fellow graziers had persuaded him into a spectacular business venture that had crashed by the time Susan was ten years old. They had lost a fortune, but even then Grandpa had maintained them all in style until his fatal stroke. After that things got more difficult every year, though her father had slaved to hold on to his inheritance.

For a moment Susan sat her beautiful chestnut mare, seeing the golden sunshine through a mist of tears. Part of her was buried with her father. They had been so happy together. 'Two of a kind', her mother had started to say way, way back when Susan became the tomboy and Patricia the fairytale princess.

So engrossed was Susan in her memories, she failed to register the alien sound in the valley until the car was visible at last. It was moving slowly as though the driver was allowing himself plenty of time to appreciate the blessedly soothing surroundings, the peace of the countryside and the sun sinking down into the blue bowl of the hills.

The Ashtons, Susan thought, and they're early!

Again she could hear her mother's voice wailing but she was too far away from the house to ride back and warn them. Instead she would ride down and intercept the Ashtons. Heavens knows there was nothing terrible about arriving an hour earlier than expected, but her mother and Paddy minded dreadfully the 'barbarian invasions'.

By the time the car had reached the clump of

cabbage gums, Susan was in a position to admire it. It was long and low, a soft metallic silver-blue, and now she could see the insignia—a prancing horse. Let Spider think what he liked! If they could attract a few more guests who owned a Ferrari this enterprise had a real chance of getting off the ground.

Susan set off again at a fast gallop and Persian Princess, who loved nothing better, made short work of carrying her down the deep grass valley to the winding, unsealed road. There she reined in and waved and the beautiful car purred up beside her, empty save for the driver.

The sight of him rocked her, so much so she could feel herself flushing. 'Hi! May I help you?' This wasn't Tom Ashton, she just knew.

'I don't think so, sonny.' He just looked at her. 'It's the owner I'm after.'

'Then it's time we were introduced.' She spoke with such cool irony she couldn't possibly be a kid.

'I beg your pardon,' his mouth twisted. 'You must be *Miss* Drummond?'

For life, she thought angrily, if you're a sample of what a wife could expect! 'Susan Drummond,' she managed aloud, while Persian Princess reacting to her tension decided to do a little dance.

'Thorn Sinclair.' He stood out of the car and with a fearless hand instantly calmed the mare. No mean achievement, but Susan wasn't in the mood for admiring. 'Beautiful animal,' he murmured with a disconcerting change of expression. One for her. One for the mare, with Persian Princess's ears coming forward as she acknowledged the velvet caress.

'How may I help you, Mr Sinclair?' she asked in an all-too-haughty tone of voice. 'I have guests arriving shortly, so I'm rather pressed for time.'

'A full house?' Cool grey eyes swept her with mockery.

'Not this weekend.' She had absolutely no intention of dismounting. It was wonderful to look down on him when standing she wouldn't come up to his shoulder.

'Then I'm in luck.' He spoke lazily. 'Mark Greenfield recommended this place to me.'

'You're in need of a quiet weekend?' she answered acidly.

'Relaxation, Miss Drummond, is important.'

'I'm afraid. . .'

'I'm here, Miss Drummond,' he said, and his silver eyes narrowed. 'I'm also quite prepared to pay you for any extra trouble.'

She had never been more conscious of her appearance in her life, hating his amused insolence, the air of arrogance and command. He wasn't handsome. He had a hump at the bridge of his nose and a deep cleft in that jutting jaw, but she supposed most people would find him impressive. In addition to his height and breadth of shoulder he had a very irritating aura of power, like a leopard who could never change his spots.

'Well, little one?'

It was obvious he considered her something of a joke, so she said in a remote, considering voice, 'How long would you want to stay?'

'A few days. Could I rely on you for a few days?'

She wanted to *hit* him! It was incredible. She always saw herself as a very civilised person, yet if she had had a crop in her hand it would have taken her all her time not to swish it across his extraordinary face.

'I seem to have thrown you off balance.' His

fingers were now on the reins. 'Are you sure I can't speak with your mother?'

'You'd better stand back from Persian Princess,' Susan said too evenly. 'She's very temperamental.'

'You're the one who's angry.'

Please, please, God, keep me calm. 'Of course I'm not angry,' she denied, with even her blood molten. 'I just can't delay any more. If you'll drive up to the house, Mr Sinclair, I'm sure we can work out something. You're quite welcome to park your car in the family garage to the rear of the house. I imagine you'd like it under cover.'

'Thank you.' He turned away from her with careless arrogance. 'This is wonderful hospitality.'

She just couldn't wait around any more. Touching the mare with her heels, she all but flew away while the man called Thorn Sinclair leaned against the side of his blue car and watched them with amusement in his eyes.

She dismounted almost furiously and threw the reins at Spider, who had found his way up to the house.

'We've got another visitor.'

'Car sure is different!' Spider said in some awe. 'I never seen a car quite like that before.'

'I've got to tell the family.'

'It'll be okay, Susie,' Spider tried to soothe her, noticing the flushed cheeks and the sparkling eyes. 'Good ole Annie could soothe any man with one of her meals.'

'Good grief, isn't this unusual?' Julia Drummond protested when she heard the news. 'You mean he's here now?'

'Yes, and I'll have to go.'

'Don't expect me to appear at dinner,' Patricia warned, without hesitation. 'Who knows what kind of person you've allowed into our house!'

Thorn Sinclair was standing in the entrance hall looking around him with all the academic interest of an architect or a builder. 'A beautiful place you have here.' The cool eyes reflected on her altered appearance minus the low-slung, wide-brimmed hat.

'You sound surprised?' She tried to be smooth, but it was a tremendous effort.

'Not at all. There's a whole legend built around Cobalt Downs.'

'I know.' She looked away from him and her voice sank. 'I'm sorry there's no one here to carry your bag.'

'Except one little female who has taken an instant dislike to me.'

'I want to like you, Mr Sinclair,' she said.

'After all, you've got to.'

She heard the laughter in his voice. 'Would you like to come this way.' She gestured towards the beautiful, romantic stairway with one hand. 'There's really nowhere that's out of bounds except our private wing.'

'How long have you been doing this?' he asked, as he came after her.

'Eighteen months.' He was the most different man she had ever known. Usually she got on very well with the opposite sex because she liked them, but this man she didn't like at all. He stirred her up in a highly disturbing way.

'You mean you started when you were still at school?'

'I'm twenty, Mr Sinclair!' She swung back at him and came up breathless, even in her agitation shrinking back a little.

'So old?'

'Old enough to run this place.' Oh hell!

'You have staff?'

She said nothing until she had opened up his door. 'Of course.'

'Who can't be found.' He walked past her and looked around. Without quite knowing what she was doing she had somehow given him her grandfather's old room. After all, he was a big man and even if he was a villain the room seemed to suit him.

'You surprise me, Miss Drummond,' he said. 'I wasn't expecting such grandeur.'

'It's a big room and you're a big man. You don't have to have it if you don't like it.'

'I beg your pardon. I couldn't admire it more.'

She wasn't sure if it was sardonic charm or outright mockery, so she walked to the french doors that led out on to the balcony with the intention of opening them out. The view from the front of the house was her favourite, with the fountain playing.

'Please, let me.'

She gave in at once, drawing back against the wall. His fingers had only brushed against hers, but the confusion in her brain was extraordinary. The very thought of it made her angry and frightened.

'For Pete's sake,' he said rather shortly, 'I won't hurt you.'

It was all getting terribly out of hand. Susan slipped past him as calmly as she could indicating the extraordinarily beautiful view. 'I've never ever decided which time of day I prefer, dawn or sunset.'

'We're certainly looking at quite a picture now. Stop playing the little proprietress for a moment and relax.'

'I don't know that I can,' she turned away from him. 'I'm expecting other guests very shortly.'

'So it turns out they haven't arrived in the valley. We have a splendid vantage-point from here.'

In the late afternoon the western sky was a glory, and Susan went to stand beside him looking out over the green valley that ruled her life. She could not, would not, accept that its halcyon days were over forever.

'This is wonderfully unspoiled country,' he murmured. 'Absolutely perfect.'

'*I* love it.'

'Beyond reason, I think.'

Was he not to pass through the ordinary stages of communication but strike at the heart? She turned her small, shapely head and looked straight at him. 'Is it so unusual, Mr Sinclair, to want to hold on to one's birthright?'

'It might come overpriced,' he pointed out.

'You're a stranger to this valley,' she said coldly.

'I already know a great deal about it. About you.'

'You thought I was a boy.'

'I don't now.' His silver-grey eyes looked down at her gleaming curls, the small fine-boned face, the short nose and the tender mouth, the angry flash in her beautiful, clear green eyes. She was a small girl and very slender, but her body was as beautifully shaped as any man could wish for, the tilt of her breasts clearly outlined against her thin cotton shirt.

What struck her immediately was how unbearably conscious he made her of her own body. No one had ever looked at her quite like that before, and if she knew she wasn't a knockout like Patricia she had nevertheless had more than her share of admiring glances. The flood of heat that surged through her veins confounded her and she moved away from the white wrought-iron railing towards the french doors. 'Dinner is at seven,' she said, 'if that suits you. We haven't discussed the tariff. . . .'

'And we don't have to.' An odd note settled into his voice, a kind of hard impatience. He frowned suddenly and it was exquisitely disturbing, a warning. Who was he, for Pete's sake? Needless to say, rich and important. It was all over him like an extra garment. 'Just write me up the bill when I leave.'

'Which is when?' she asked.

'I'm not sure. At least a few days.'

'Very well.' Her voice was flat and very cool. 'If there's anything at all you need, please let me know. You have a dressing room and a private bath just through that door.'

'Thank you, Miss Drummond,' he said. 'I can't wait to meet your family.'

CHAPTER TWO

'So we've got an extra guest?' Annie snorted in the kitchen.

'He's a bastard!' muttered Susan.

'What's that?' Annie almost dropped a loaf of bread. 'It's not like you to swear.'

'I'm swearing this time.'

'But, Susan,' Annie was so perturbed she stopped work, 'why did you agree to take him on? We can't have any uncivilised folk here.'

'I don't mean he's uncivilised,' Susan said. 'I mean he's the most . . . provoking man.'

'What could he possibly say to upset you?' Annie asked. She took up a carving knife.

'Nothing really.' Susan's small face looked perplexed, she gave a little laugh that came out faintly strangled. 'I'd say he was an expert at unsettling people. He's big and tall and formidable, I suppose. I can't handle him, as it happens. He alternates between being curt and charming.'

'You've got me really worried,' said Annie, shaking her head. 'Where is he now?'

'Settling in. I gave him Grandpa's old room.'

'You *what*?' Annie started to sponge furiously at the sink. 'This isn't making sense.'

'He's not the sort of person you would think of giving anything but the best.'

'That's easy to see!' Annie asserted. 'Whatever made you give him your grandpa's room?'

'I told you.' Susan looked very young and vulnerable.

'Then you must respect him.'

'I hate him, I think.'

'At first sight?' Annie looked seriously shocked.

'I don't come up against people like that very often,' Susan excused herself. 'He wants to stay for a few days.'

'Did he tell you why?' Annie obviously didn't know whether to be glad or sorry.

'He said he wants to relax, but he doesn't look the sort of man who ever relaxes. He's sort of high-mettled.'

'I'm tempted to go up and introduce myself,' Annie said. 'We need to get this thing straightened out before we let him stay.'

'Oh, don't be silly, Annie,' Susan gave a little, nervous laugh. 'He's perfectly respectable. I just can't find the right word to describe him.'

'You tried one,' Annie cut in ominously.

'I only meant he's sarcastic.'

'I have an excuse,' said Annie. 'I'll take linen up to his room.'

'The bed's made.'

'Extra pillows.'

She was stopped in the act of doing just that by Patricia's flying entrance into the kitchen.

'What's wrong?' Susan swung around, enquiring. Patricia rarely visited the kitchen.

'I want our guest's name!' said Patricia excitedly.

'Why?' Susan was more than ever flustered.

'I want to *know*!' Patricia snapped back. 'For the first time ever you've got someone I'd actually like to meet.'

'Really?' Annie, too, was staring at Patricia in astonishment.

'Whatever is the matter with you two?' Patricia looked back at them with exasperation. 'I've just spotted the most gorgeous man I've ever seen in my life walking in our garden, and I'm quite sure I would like to speak to him tonight. I'm sure Mummy would too. He's most emphatically a gentleman.'

'Susy doesn't seem to think so,' said Annie.

'I doubt Susan would know.'

'Wouldn't she?' Annie eyed the older girl belligerently. 'Susan is an excellent judge.'

'I don't think of clever, sophisticated men.' Patricia was looking very pretty and flushed. 'What's his name, Sue, and what does he *do*?'

Susan gave in. 'His name is Thorn Sinclair and I didn't think to ask him what line of business he was in. I'm sure he's not a doctor or some trustworthy person like that.'

'Not to worry!' Patricia smiled. 'I'll find out.'

For some reason Annie took objection to this. 'Why didn't you tell me he was handsome?' she demanded.

'He's *not* handsome!' Susan protested in some amazement. 'I think his nose has been broken at some time, and I'm not surprised.'

'Patricia seems prepared to grab him,' Annie muttered a bit pointedly. 'Why not put on a pretty dress tonight?'

'To impress Mr Sinclair?' Susan asked incredulously. 'As it happens, he mistook me for a boy— and how do we know he hasn't got a beautiful wife tucked away some place?'

'Inasmuch as he never thought to bring her. Most men bring their wives, don't you agree?'

'He's probably divorced. Mental cruelty. Anyway, I'm off to see if the rest of our guests have settled in. As it now stands, we have an unlucky thirteen.'

She drove down to the creek that was now festooned with blue and yellow tents along the bank and in a few moments she was joined by the campers.

'How's it going?' she asked them.

Everyone seemed to answer at once, adults and children, until Bob Irving separated himself from the rest and ran through a string of names.

'A beautiful property you have here, Miss Drummond,' he told her with enthusiasm.

'And that's a smashing house!' a little boy seconded, to a gale of hilarity. 'How much did it cost?'

'A great deal of money a long time ago,' Susan conferred a smile on him. 'It's probably much too big for most people.'

'A wonderful idea of yours,' Bob Irving told her firmly. 'We can help you, and in turn you can offer us magnificent camping grounds. All the kids are so excited I expect they won't sleep.'

'Oh, I think they will!' Susan ruffled the hair of a small child looking up at her. 'It's very soothing sleeping out under the stars.'

'And we're going canoeing tomorrow,' she was told.

'Sounds exciting!'

'Would you like to see inside our tent?' the little girl asked her, while her mother pointed out hastily that Miss Drummond was busy.

'Yes, I would.'

'Daddy let us help him put it up.' Susan allowed herself to be led away and in the end spent more time at the camping ground than she actually intended. She had yet to shower and change, then race down to the kitchen to help Annie. Her good intentions often got her into trouble, but it wasn't easy to walk away from the children who were so excited and full of talk. At least some of her guests appreciated lovely country—but then she remembered that in spite of the clamour Thorn Sinclair

had aroused in her too had responded to the
special atmosphere. He had an excellent voice,
deep and vibrant, and he used it as an instrument
of power, letting the colour and inflection change.
Look at the way he had murmured to the mare! So
he knew how to talk to horses. It was the only
good point in his favour.

She was just about to take her shower when her
mother came through the door. 'Goodness, Susan,
you're way behind the rest of us!'

'You look lovely, Mamma. Are you coming
down to dinner?'

'Are you telling me what to do in my own
house?'

'Of course I'm not!' Susan looked disconcerted.
'It's only that . . .'

'I don't usually appear?'

'Yes.'

'I'm doing it as a courtesy to Mr Sinclair.'

'You've met him?'

'I have. A pity you couldn't have been on hand. I
have a right to meet our guests.'

'I had to check on the other people, Mamma.'

'He seems a very striking man,' said Julia, her
eyes bright. 'Has he said what sort of . . . job he's
in?'

'No. The only thing that seems clear is it's
profitable. He drives a very splendiferous car,
though that doesn't automatically give him a good
character.'

'One has only to look at him to see he has
character,' Julia announced. 'What *is* Annie giving
us for dinner?'

'Trust her, Mamma, it will be something
delicious.'

'I think I'll go and check. We're serving wine, I
suppose. Go down to the cellar and bring up some

we've been keeping. You know the right years—your father made sure you knew that kind of thing. Why, I was never sure. And Susan,' her mother turned back to her, 'please change into something suitable. I don't want you looking like the poor relation.'

Now that's going to be a problem, Susan thought. She covered her hair with a cap and dashed under the warm shower, allowing it to run cold so her skin tingled.

'Something suitable!' she said aloud when she was back in her bedroom. 'I only wish I could oblige.'

Finally she made her selection, standing poised like a deer in front of her mirror. A ruffled skirt sprinkled with flowers, peasant style, a sheer white blouse trimmed with cream lace. It needed a bit of drama, so she picked up a long silk scarf in an emerald green and sashed it around her. There, that was better! She supposed she *did* look like a gipsy—black hair, golden skin, startling green eyes. If Patricia was a lovely watercolour, she supposed she was a flamboyant oil.

While her father was alive, it had never seemed so hurtful, the open favouritism her mother showed, but these days she was feeling wounded. Perhaps she shouldn't care so much. She had certainly been her father's girl, but it was an unspoken thing, a special empathy that never, ever, left Patricia out in the cold. That would have been unthinkable. There had been no jealous competition between them for their father's attention. He had related to both his daughters in such a wise and loving way there had never been any cause for either to feel hurt or rejected—an achievement really, because Paddy had a jealous nature.

Susan could her the voices as she was coming down the stairway; that man Sinclair and Patricia's. She was laughing and it sounded very pretty. Susan hesitated on the bottom of the stairs, then she supposed she had better make an appearance, a brief one before she went to help Annie.

'Good evening,' she said, poised in the double doorway, her eyes on the animated little group.

'Good evening.' Thorn Sinclair stood up and Julia set her glass of sherry down and turned to smile at her younger daughter. 'Ah, there you are, dear.'

'We were just trying to find out where Mr Sinclair comes from,' Patricia said jokingly. She was wearing her white pleated silk dress and her long blonde hair hung loose and shining. She looked happy and excited, and even her mother, so often pale and stiff these days, looked younger and softer, obviously enjoying the unexpected company of such an attractive man; though attractive didn't say it. His looks and personality were far too strong. He had changed his clothes, striking just the right note between casual and formal. A charcoal fine-checked jacket, grey trousers, pearl grey cotton shirt with the finest self-stripe, a burgundy silk cravat loosely tied at the bronzed throat. It was all rather splendid yet completely uncontrived.

'Would you like a drink, dear?' her mother asked.

'No, thanks, Mummy. I'll see if Annie needs a hand.' Inside the kitchen Annie was fuming. 'This Mr Sinclair must *really* be something.'

'What's wrong, Annie?' Susan placed a hand on Annie's plump arm.

'For pity's sake!' Annie's face was flushed. 'I've had your mother in here running around like a general. She hasn't shown her face in here for years—now there was absolutely nothing right for dinner.'

'Impossible with you, Annie.' Susan tried to jolly her out of it. 'You know how Mamma is. She just fusses sometimes.'

'If it wasn't for you, my girl, I'd clear out!'

'Oh, don't say that, Annie!' Susan just barely suppressed a sob. 'What did Mamma say?'

'She was critical of everything on the menu,' Annie said, still looking extremely annoyed. 'Anyone would think it was Prince Charles!'

'So surely we're having what we were having this morning?'

'We are. Mushroom soup—and not the tinned variety either. Beef Wellington, and no one can beat the beef or my puff pastry, and a good old English trifle. Not good enough, it seems.'

'You're a great cook, Annie. I'm sure our guests will be well satisfied. They always have been.'

'It should have been haute cuisine,' Annie snorted, fracturing the French. 'A vichyssoise followed by boeuf à la something with pommes au beurre and some petits pots de chocolat à la mango.'

'I fell in love with the Beef Wellington,' Susan said. 'Mamma didn't mean anything, Annie. It's just that Mr Sinclair has a powerful effect on everybody.'

'Isn't that clear!' Annie banged a cupboard door. 'Don't take any notice of me, love. I just feel all smashed up.'

'Oh, Annie—all these years and you've been so wonderful! It's that man Sinclair's fault, not Mamma's. She just wants to impress him.'

'She wants to impress him all right,' Annie agreed grimly. 'I see Patricia has her best dress on.'

'She looks ravishing,' Susan smiled. 'I don't know why they're both so taken with Mr Sinclair. He frightens and confuses me.'

'Well, I guess I'll get to meet him some time.'

'As soon as we walk out this door. Now tell me what to do.'

'You can whip the cream, m'darlin'. I've got everything else under control.'

'Of course.' Susan searched out a mixing bowl. 'Mamma wants me to bring up some wine from the cellar. I'd better do it now. The white will have to be chilled and the red given time to breathe. I should have done it sooner—the cellar is cold.'

'Surely you're not opening the good stuff?' Annie seemed to be finding everything vastly disturbing.

'Mamma wants it.'

'And what Mamma wants, Mamma gets.' Annie attempted unsuccessfully to hide her increasing lack of good feeling towards Julia Drummond. They had never got on very well as Annie quite failed to know her place, but while John Drummond was alive the atmosphere at Cobalt Downs was most pleasant. Now everything had changed. Despite the fact that Annie was only drawing money for necessities, simply because of family loyalty and her love for Susan, Julia had embarked on a course of high-toned aggression. Even for Susan it couldn't last.

I'll have to speak to Mamma, Susan thought. How can we possibly get along without Annie? However could Mamma attack her? Looking at the flushed, dreadfully upset face, Susan knew an agony of protective love. Annie was family. She was also growing old. Surely Mamma realised that?

Downstairs in the cellar Susan searched quickly for a few bottles of wine, quickly found them, and took them back upstairs. Grandpa had always maintained an excellent, balanced cellar and both he and her father had acted as senior judges in wine shows for many years, so undeterred, Susan picked up the best; a rare Riesling because her mother only drank white wine, a beautiful Cabernet Sauvignon that would have reached perfection in the bottle and the justly famous Drummond Tawny Port, named after her grandfather. She had the certain feeling that Mr Sinclair would appreciate it and she had every intention of putting it all down on his bill.

Dinner was almost a gala. The Ashtons were a very pleasant middle-aged couple who cherished these quiet, unspoiled weekends and given a little encouragement and their fair share of wine added more and more to the swirl of conversation. It appeared they were almost as widely travelled as Mr Sinclair, who although he told them a great deal about what was interesting and entertaining, failed to tell them anything of himself.

It was a very cordial affair indeed, with a kind of glow hanging over Julia and her elder daughter. Susan to a large extent was forced out of the sparkling conversation because of her need to assist Annie, and although the guests looked at her from time to time, in particular, Thorn Sinclair, Julia and Patricia were gently unaware, perhaps even ashamed of Susan's comings and goings.

'Well, what do you think of him?' Susan couldn't resist asking Annie as soon as she was able.

'I wonder if he's married?' queried Annie.

'If he is he's keeping it a secret.' Susan switched on the percolater. 'I haven't seen Mamma and Paddy so happy and animated in years. She mustn't fall in love with him—that would be terrible. He's going away in a few days.'

'I wouldn't let a man like that get by.' Annie was still basking in the smile he had given her.

'Impossible— you *like* him!' Susan turned her head, looking slightly betrayed.

'I don't know him, darlin'.' Annie spoke calmly. 'But there's no denyin' he's a very fine-lookin' man.'

'So Paddy better keep on asking questions, and yet I think I'd be appalled if she got involved with that man. He's not *gentle*!'

'Something about him threatens you,' Annie murmured wisely. 'Did you see the way he finished up my Beef Wellington? Now there's a man who appreciates good food!'

The Ashtons went for an after-dinner stroll beneath the gloriously blossoming stars and not long after, to Julia's intense pleasure, Patricia sold Mr Sinclair on the idea. Julia had been in a frenzy of matchmaking since Mr Sinclair, apparently overcome by pity, had given away the fact he was a bachelor.

'A good dinner. A very good evening!' she told Susan smilingly as Susan was putting the long mahogany dinner table to rights. The Victorian Gothic dining chairs were very heavy, so she left four along the wall while she struggled with the magnificent antique silver candelabra and the even more impressive silver centrepiece that had adorned the dining room table for as long as she could remember. Susan was passionately attached to everything in the house, though the size of it and the very many inherited possessions made for a lot of work. All the rooms by modern standards were immense and many of the original wallpapers in the house, though very beautiful, badly needed replacing, as did the floral chintz curtains and slip covers in the drawing room. In the old days there had been many servants and magnificent parties, but all that was over. Why, she couldn't even get at the cobwebs on the very high ceilings, and Annie had long since given up the endless polishing and dusting.

'How old would you say Mr Sinclair is?' Julia asked suddenly.

'Thirty-four or five.'

'He was very taken with Patricia, wasn't he?'

'I'm afraid I didn't notice, Mamma.'

'Well, he *was*.' Julia answered shortly. 'How embarrassing it was, Susan, your jumping up and down!'

'Someone had to help Annie.' Susan looked at her mother incredulously. 'We can't expect her to do it all on her own. As a matter of fact, we're expecting far too much of her already.'

'In what way?' Julia's voice had an accusing ring to it.

'Mamma, you must be joking! Annie doesn't ask for a penny for weeks on end. I feel her sacrifices on your behalf very deeply.'

'Surely she's free to go!' Julia said.

'*Go?*' Susan's clear voice lost its gentle note. 'Annie lives here! She's family!'

'Rubbish! She's been in service to this family.' Julia's long-held resentments were coming out. 'To be frank, I'm surprised she hasn't spoken of retiring. I had rather an unpleasant incident with her earlier this evening. She's always been encouraged to say and do as she liked, but I've never gone on about it up until now. *I* am mistress here.'

'Daddy referred to Annie specifically in his will.' Susan realised she had to be very careful. 'Annie has been part of Cobalt Downs since she came here as a young girl. She has nowhere else, no family but us. She can be outspoken, I know, but she's given everything of herself to this family, all her love and loyalty and energy. I'll always look after Annie.'

'Obviously your father realised you might *have* to,' Julia cut in rather bitterly. 'You have the controlling vote on what happens to this property, Susan, but I'm beginning to think you're making problems for all of us. Patricia is a very beautiful girl, she should be out in the world instead of sitting here in a run-down old mansion. I'm even terrified to ask you if we mightn't sell a picture.'

'Do you want to sell one, Mamma?' Susan asked.

'Why not? I have Patricia to think about. She's twenty-four years old and despite her charm and beauty no one is rushing to marry her. Because she's hidden!'

'Perhaps you'd like a holiday?' Susan sank down on the Gothic chair beside the wall. 'We can sell a picture if you want to, Mamma. I'll do anything you want—you know that.'

'Except put Cobalt Downs on the market?'

'I swore to Daddy I'd hold on to it. I might even go after a rich husband.'

'You won't get one.' Julia shook her head. 'You have no idea how hard and determined you've become, how righteous about running this house, this family. Your father's will upset the whole balance. You're becoming more and more fanatical about holding on to this place. It seems you've forgotten it killed your father.'

Susan's small face stayed expressionless, though as always her heart and her stomach took a lurch. She stood up quietly and looked down at her mother. 'Decide on what painting you want to sell, Mamma, and how much you want for it. There'll be no difficulty selling. Grandpa built up a fine collection.'

'If you're really serious, my dear,' Julia said with a tight smile, 'I'll let you attend to it. I could do with a holiday and I'm sure Patricia would love it. She and Mr Sinclair are going off riding tomorrow. I'll expect you to lend her Persian Princess.'

'She'll unseat her, Mamma,' Susan protested.

'Nonsense! Patricia will have no difficulty at all.'

It was quite late when Susan stole back into the kitchen to finish the washing up. Only so much went in the dishwasher, and Annie had looked so spent Susan had acted with enormous diplomacy to hurry her off to bed. Now at last the house was quiet, so she could rattle around downstairs to her heart's content. The Ashtons had wanted her to know how much they had enjoyed dinner in such delightful company and told her they intended taking a long walk before breakfast. Mr Ashton, a business executive, had suffered a mild heart attack some months before and his doctor had recommended lots of relaxing breaks and long, easy walks. Cobalt Downs boasted plenty of them, and early morning in the valley was a time and a place to be calm in.

There was a hole in one of Annie's rubber gloves and Susan threw them off with disgust. She tried as much as she could to protect her hands, nevertheless she wasn't too proud of them. For a long moment she stood looking down at them, small and finely boned like the rest of her but with the nails clipped boyishly short and a large blister between the thumb and first finger of her left hand. There were a few callouses as well on the padded palm. Ah, well!

'What the devil are you doing there?'

The vehemence of the tone shocked her, and she spun around, knowing the need to protect herself. 'Mr. Sinclair! For Pete's sake, you frightened me!'

'I'm sorry.' He advanced into the kitchen, reducing its large dimensions to the claustrophobic closeness of a cupboard. 'I thought you might have been warned by my footsteps.'

'Unfortunately no.' Susan stood with her back to the double sink. 'Can I help you?'

'Surely it's the other way around?' He was frowning, his grey eyes studying her face intently.

'I'm just finishing off, that's all.'

'And what time is that? Around dawn?'

'I'm not in the least tired,' she assured him.

'You look it.' To her dismay he put out his hand and just barely brushed the smudged shadows beneath her eyes. 'I thought I heard sounds down here.'

'I wasn't making any noise.'

'I have very acute hearing—besides, I couldn't possibly go to sleep so early.'

'But it's nearly midnight!'

'So?' He gave her what might have been on someone else, a charming teasing smile. 'I don't require too many hours' sleep.'

'Then you must be a late riser,' commented Susan.

'You're very tense, aren't you?'

'I suppose I seem so,' she said with a short sigh. 'If you'd like to read, we have a very grand library, but nothing terribly up to date. I used to be an inveterate reader, but I never seem to get the time any more.'

'You don't mind this slavery?' He took up a tea-towel and started to dry the dishes.

'You don't have to do that,' she protested.

'My dear child, it's very heartwarming to see so much spunk, but you'll never get through at this rate. Why don't you ask your enchanting sister to give you a hand?'

'Patricia does her share.'

'Really? With pink nails out to here?'

'You don't have to worry,' she said.

'Still hating me?' he asked, so boldly it took her breath away.

'I have a surprise for you, Mr Sinclair,' she said coldly. 'You haven't bothered me at all.'

'You just look so apprehensive every time I appear.'

'Probably I'm wondering exactly what you're doing here.' She turned her head and allowed her eyes to rest briefly on his face. 'You don't seem the type for country weekends, unless there was plenty of polo laid on—and you said yourself you're a night owl.'

'So how did you know I played polo?' he asked.

'Don't you?' She looked defiantly back at him.

'Yes, I do. Smart girl!'

'So what *are* you here for, Mr Sinclair?'

'Would you believe in search of peace?'

'No.' Susan looked at him and her green eyes were sparkling. 'I have a feeling you're in search of something that's going to totally alter our lives.'

'You seem to be uncommonly psychic?'

'Not at all. You just have a hard and calculating look.'

'And you have a very sharp tongue. It's fascinating—a little bit of nothing ticking me off!'

'And you're accustomed to people who probably bend the knee.'

'Speaking of knees, you might find yourself over one in a minute!' he warned.

'Because I'm a woman?'

'God love you, you're a child!'

'Who knows what she wants. If you've got something on your mind, Mr Sinclair, you'd better pack up and go home.'

'At least not until I've finished the washing up,' he insisted.

'I notice you haven't contradicted me?'

'Perhaps I'm playing for time. Your sister asked me to go riding with her in the morning.'

'Lovely. It's rather quiet for Patricia.'

'And damn near exhausting for you.'

'Well, I'm sure you don't want *me* to go riding with you!' Susan retorted.

'When you ride as well as a jockey.'

'If you're very good I'll show you my ribbons.'

'I already know about your exploits in the show ring. I've even seen a photograph of you someplace—Miss Susan Drummond on Brigadoon and underneath eulogies of praise. It was hard to say who looked sweeter, you or the chestnut.'

'That was my father's favourite photograph of me,' she said. 'He had it blown up so he could hang it in his study.'

'You loved your father very much,' Thorn Sinclair said quietly.

'Love is sometimes an inadequate word. It's used so freely when in fact a lot of people don't know it at all.'

'Sad but true, especially in the family context. But sexual love can be a madness.'

'I wouldn't know.' She let the water out and dried her hands.

'Honestly, you didn't have to answer.'

She had a small dilemma on her hands because he had her pinned at the kitchen sink. 'Well, that's the way it is, Mr Sinclair.' She tilted her delicately determined chin. 'Which reminds me—I wouldn't like to see my sister suffer because of your visit.'

'Miss Drummond, you say the wildest things!'

Susan found herself leaning back further. 'Except that I saw you turning your very experienced charm on her. We haven't had the opportunity to lead a glamorous life here.'

'And you think I might dazzle your sister?'

'Unintentionally, of course.'

'But it doesn't hold good for you?'

'I have felt the odd flutter,' she said tautly, 'but that's simply because we lead such a quiet life.'

'You're trembling.' He was cool, half smiling, half hostile.

'You're rather good at intimidation.'

'I'm also tempted to be fool enough to kiss you.'

'And why would you do that?' She felt a shock wave of panic jolt through her.

'Because it would hurt.'

'It would.' She made a wry little face and bit her lip. 'I think we're even now, Mr Sinclair. Would you mind not towering over me? It makes me feel like a cat with a bird.'

'You're the cat, green eyes.' He moved away from her with languid ease. 'You'll have to sweeten that tongue before you have half a chance of finding a husband.'

'And what's wrong with being a solitary spinster?' she charged him. 'It seems a man can remain single and desirable his whole life long, but being called a spinster is meant to leave a bitter taste. Well, *I* don't think so.'

'And I don't either.' He suddenly swung on her, put his two hands beneath her rib cage and lifted her on to the counter beside the sink. 'Let's face it, little one. You're bugging me, and I don't like that.'

'I'm sorry.' It was a sense of danger that made her apologise. He was very tall, very strong and very alert.

'You know perfectly well you're *not* sorry,' he taunted her, 'but it's no bad thing if you've got the sense to be afraid.'

Her green eyes, huge and intense, registered a mixture of emotions. 'I can't imagine what we're doing here like this.'

Thorn Sinclair shrugged his wide shoulders. 'It

happens sometimes. Something goes badly wrong at first sight.'

'Well, thanks for wiping up.' Her stiff little tone was oddly poignant.

'I've heard a lot of things in the town,' he added.

'What sort of things?' Instantly she was back to hostility.

'Oh, mostly admiration. How you're battling to keep this place.'

'And you think I'm a fool.'

'On the contrary,' the silver-grey eyes studied her with more insolence than admiration, 'I think it's quite a good idea, but you're hopelessly under-capitalised let alone under-staffed.'

'Give me time!' Her chin came up.

'Does your brother never come home?'

Susan looked away from him swiftly, hating his hard, glittering look. 'Of course he does—as often as he's able. He's going to be a doctor.'

'And you're going to run a guesthouse. For how long?'

'What's it got to do with you?' she challenged, with a decided show of spirit.

'Maybe I wouldn't like to see that fine jaunty spirit go under. You're lucky you have ... Annie, isn't it? But you appear to be up against your mother and sister. Patricia talked a good deal tonight.'

'You mean you led her on?'

'Just verbally, Susan.'

'I'm sorry, I almost prefer Sonny,' she said waspishly.

'I beg of you, Miss Drummond,' he said suavely. 'Forgive me. I don't expect you to ride around like a high priestess of fashion.'

'I'm tired,' she managed, just above a whisper.

'It's been a long day.'

'I can believe it.' He gave an odd, brief laugh. 'You go up. I'll check on everything down here.'

What happened then seemed to happen in slow motion, with no sense of reality at all. He lifted her and quite without volition she slumped against him, dizzy with tiredness and accumulated tensions.

At first he steadied her, then when it became apparent her legs would not support her, he held her tightly, propped up against him, all but taking her slight weight.

'Are you all right?' His voice had lost that urbane drawl.

'Yes ' In fact she was stunned by their closeness, mind and body trembling as she encountered the full force of his magnetic attraction.

He tilted her head back, just by holding her head in his hand. 'There's something very dangerous about innocence.'

Susan shook her head, trying desperately to refute this, crazy unwanted intimacy. 'Please ... I'm all right now.'

'Don't all little girls get kissed goodnight?' He held her eyes with his.

'Not this one.'

'Even when you're full of tears?'

His eyes were pure silver in the lamplight, too worldly, too knowing, living diamonds. She meant to say something, deny it—anything, but even her tongue seemed paralysed, and as she continued to stare back at him, her eyes wide and unusually darkened, he lowered his dark head and covered her soft mouth with his own.

The shock of it was immense, like an earthquake, and immediately she grew fainter, not even capable as she wanted, of keeping her lips

tightly closed. They might have been petals of a
flower, opening ... opening ... so he could enter
into the very centre of sweetness.

Possession. Previously it had only been a word.

When finally he released her, she had to take
several quick shallow breaths, clinging to him until
the roaring in her ears subsided. She had been
kissed before and often very pleasurably, but this
was the first time she had ever experienced aching
torment, ever known herself capable of a
terrifying, unwilling surrender.

Her heart was pounding and sensations were
radiating from the very centre of her being,
sparkling in her blood, causing spasms of
excitement all over her body. It was so strange and
so powerful she wanted to cry out. Indeed, she did
give a husky, little moan.

'If you'll just let me *go*!'

His eyes narrowed over her, but his voice was
quiet. 'Are you sure you can stand?'

'You shouldn't have done that, Mr Sinclair,' she
said ridiculously, but his face wore such a look of
sensuality it nearly stopped her heart.

'And you shouldn't have bothered me, Miss
Drummond,' he returned with suave reason-
ableness.

It was useless to pursue it, she knew. What was
a most serious matter for her was only a minute's
diversion for him. He was probably used to high-
voltage affairs with experienced, sophisticated
women, whereas she had just received her first
insight into passion.

Belatedly she broke away from him and fled
across the room, body and brain in so much
confusion she scarcely knew what she was doing.
Damn him—*damn him*! he had rendered her a
helpless puppet. 'Are you ready?' she asked

carefully, one hand going to the light switch.

'For what?' He came towards her with quite natural assured grace, and once again she was robbed of a breathing space.

'To go upstairs, of course.' Heat seemed to be flooding her body, colouring her skin.

He stared back at her with a blandly, mocking face. 'Quite frankly, Miss Drummond, I'd like to take you with me, only I'd be dead tomorrow from the shame.'

His meaning took a few seconds to reach her fully and then she gasped in outrage. 'And you think I'd go?'

He laughed, unkindly. 'I think I could pick you up and carry you off this minute.'

'Then try it!' she snapped at him with an onrush of pure rage.

'Magnificent!' Unforgivably he laughed at her. 'From a beautiful, bemused little virgin to a spitting kitten.' He studied the wild flush on her cheeks. 'Did you know your eyes go from a clear green to a deep emerald?'

But Susan was beyond diverting. 'I'm more aware you're a . . . bit of a scoundrel!' she said angrily, luxuriating in the accusation.

'Scoundrel?' He tested the word in amazement. 'My dear girl, *who* quite literally threw herself into my arms?'

'I didn't know I had!'

'Well, you did,' he corrected her coolly. 'And I've always been a man to take advantage of a situation once it presents itself.'

'I believe it!' Even the lift of his eyebrow infuriated her beyond belief.

'Good, then be warned.'

It seemed that all of a sudden her whole life was being taken out of her control. 'Of course you mean to try much the same thing tomorrow,' she challenged him bitterly.

'Now that's my business, Susan,' he told her smoothly. 'You obviously think your sister is the beauty of the family, but believe me, she hasn't got your sex appeal.'

'I wouldn't believe you about anything!' She stared at him with enormous, over-wrought eyes.

'The animosity is mutual.' Thorn Sinclair inclined his arrogant, dark head. 'I suppose you won't rest until I apologise for calling you sonny?'

'Oh, listen, please, I'm very tired.'

'Then go to bed.' His hand came out and unexpectedly he smoothed the dark curls from her forehead. 'Did I hurt you?'

'No, you didn't.'

'But I surprised you about yourself?'

Didn't he know he nearly had her crying? 'In what way?' She was nearly floating with exhausted emotion.

'You've never been so aware of a man, have you? Of yourself?'

It wasn't until she was safely alone in her bedroom that Susan allowed herself to admit it.

CHAPTER THREE

'DIDN'T you sleep, love?' Annie asked her anxiously next morning.

'Tossed and turned all night.' Susan slipped on to a high chair and began the bowl of muesli Annie had set before her.

'The Ashtons have gone walking.' Determinedly Annie added a boiled egg and toast she had already buttered. 'Eat it, my girl.'

'They're nice people, aren't they?' Susan murmured. 'So are our campers at the creek. The children asked me if they might see over the house.'

'Your mother won't like that, darlin',' Annie warned her.

'I suppose if I ask the children I would have to ask their parents,' said Susan a shade unhappily.

'No, I don't think so.' Briskly Annie made the decision. 'People pay to either camp on the property or stay at the house. It might be better not to involve yourself with the children. I know you find it hard to refuse youngsters, but your mother finds our visitors a nightmare.'

'*Not* Mr Sinclair,' Susan said.

'I'm impressed myself,' Annie chuckled. 'He'll probably meet up with the Ashtons. He went for an early morning walk himself.'

'Then I suppose it's safe to enjoy my breakfast.'

'What do you suppose he's doing here?' Annie asked.

'I wish I knew.' Absentmindedly Susan drank a glass of milk. 'He's scarcely our usual kind of guest.'

'He's not usual at all.' Annie took sausages and fillet steak from the refrigerator. 'You don't suppose he's a developer, do you?'

'I think he's casing the joint, as they say.'

'Um.' Annie frowned earnestly. 'He looks rich.'

'A lord of creation!' Susan muttered, with unaccustomed passion. 'If he *is* a developer he's wasting his time, I'm afraid.'

'Patricia has taken a shine to him,' Annie remarked without meeting Susan's eye.

'That kind of man could only make a woman suffer,' Susan replied, after a long silence.

'Well, isn't that what women want?' Annie exclaimed. 'To suffer for love?'

'I wish I could tell him to go.'

'Darlin', we just can't do without the money.'

'Okay, so we'll be nice to him.'

'Well, it makes life kind of interesting,' Annie grinned. 'I haven't seen your mother and Patricia so happy in many a long day.'

'Mr Sinclair can't solve our problems,' Susan said soberly.

'Money solves a lot of problems,' said Annie. 'I wonder what he's here for?'

Such speculation, among other things, had kept Susan awake half the night. Thorn Sinclair was a very suspicious, dangerous character.

Deliberately she stayed away from the house until the breakfast period was well and truly over, but when she did venture to return it was to see Patricia and Thorn Sinclair enjoying the brilliant morning from the commanding vantage point of the four-storeyed tower.

'Hello, Susan,' Patricia called, leaning forward to wave out of the window.

'Hi there!' What else could she say?

Immediately they disappeared, and by the time

Susan walked through the handsome porte-cochère and mounted the short flight of stairs to the verandah they met up with her at the front door. Both of them were dressed in riding clothes, looking so glossy and elegant they really demanded a photograph.

'Good morning, Miss Drummond,' Thorn Sinclair looked down on her from his superior six-foot-three.

'Good morning.'

She sounded so cool and clipped Patricia looked at her with open censure. 'Get up on the wrong side of the bed this morning?'

'Can't afford to. I'm such a busy person.'

Patricia's blue eyes lightened and widened. She didn't think her sister would mention that she never got out of bed until eight or eight-thirty, but Susan's eyes were so glittery she couldn't be quite sure. 'Anyway,' Patricia said sweetly, 'we're glad you're back. Thorn and I have plans for riding around the valley.'

It struck Susan as a decided understatement. Excitement was in the air, a spring fantasy. In fact, she said very pleasantly: 'Much the best way to see it. I'm sorry we can't offer you a top-class mount, Mr Sinclair, but Mephisto should be quite acceptable.'

'Mephisto?' Patricia looked a little shaken, but held back from saying so. Mephisto was a black stallion with the proper devilish characteristics.

'A bit on the quiet side?' Thorn Sinclair asked, with a twitch of the muscle at the side of his sculptured mouth.

'An absolute pet, if he takes to you.'

'May I have Persian Princess?' Patricia interrupted. 'Mummy said I might.'

'I'd rather you didn't, Pad ... Patricia,' Susan managed. 'What about Sunshine?'

'Please, Susan,' said Patricia with gentle firmness. 'You're so possessive about everything.'

'Yes, and you know exactly why.' Susan gave her sister a level look. Persian Princess was a strong, rather impetuous ride and she didn't carry anyone at all willingly outside of her mistress, Susan. Sunshine was by far the more amenable ride, but in no way as beautiful or showy.

'Why don't you come down to the stables with us?' Thorn Sinclair suggested, 'then you can introduce me to Mephisto.'

Lanky, dreamy-eyed Spider was there before them, and when Susan told him to saddle up Mephisto for Mr Sinclair he looked at her strangely. 'Ya mean Sugar?'

'Don't tell me how he got that nickname,' Thorn Sinclair said smoothly. 'Well, come along, Spider, you don't look happy.'

'How could you know a thing like that?' Susan asked sweetly. 'Spider always looks the same.'

'I hope ya not gunna ride the Princess?' Spider gave the silent Patricia a keen look.

'For heaven's sake, why not? I'm not afraid of her.'

'She's done thrown ya once or twice.'

'*Once*,' Patricia said coldly, looking down her short, straight nose. 'Would you kindly do what you're paid to do and saddle the horses.'

Spider, who could have said a lot, said nothing. He only gave a disgusted snort and trudged off.

'I bet you're a very accomplished rider, Thorn.' Patricia looked up at that tall figure with admiring eyes.

'Clearly I'm going to have to be.' The silver-grey eyes raked Susan's innocent profile.

'Oh, here's Spider with Mephisto,' Susan cried in a bright voice, not mulling over the ethics of allowing their guest to ride an unquestionably rough and tough horse.

'Mephisto, my foot!' Thorn Sinclair surprised her by snapping. 'That's the Flying Devil, Sir Lucifer. I thought he went to stand at Gordon Lancaster's?'

'Been a real disappointment to date!' Spider was only just maintaining his balance as the rangy, high-headed thoroughbred started into his bag of tricks.

Just as he had once quietened Persian Princess, Thorn Sinclair now proceeded to take over. He walked quietly straight to the stallion and the moment he was alongside took hold of the reins. 'Easy, boy, easy!'

'Oh, *do* be careful, Thorn!' Patricia burst out. 'He can be terribly fiery.'

'And your sister told me he was charming.'

'I didn't think you'd be very enthusiastic about a thoroughly tame ride.'

'I recall Bert Morrison, the jockey, was badly injured by this horse.'

'That was years ago,' Susan said. 'They were going to geld him at the time.'

'I know.'

'You know a lot!' she snapped.

'Fortunately, Miss Drummond.'

There was no satisfaction in the thing at all. While he was talking, Thorn Sinclair vaulted into the saddle and began to walk the big stallion around the courtyard.

'Wait for it!' Spider muttered, his long, wrinkled face puckering.

'If there are any accidents, Susan,' Patricia burst out emotionally, 'I'll never forgive you!'

'Oh, be quiet!' Susan returned tartly. 'All right up there, Mr Sinclair?'

'You look magnificent!' Patricia called.

In fact he did, and Susan, who had a great craving to see him come off, was made witness to an extraordinary display. The ex-racehorse her father had nicknamed Mephisto was now being made to look like a perfect gentleman instead of the notoriously excitable blood animal that had been something of a legend on the racetracks. His hot temperament, in fact, had contributed to his premature retirement, but not before he had earned a lot of money.

At first determined on taking Persian Princess Patricia now seemed doubtful. 'I think I will take Sunshine,' she told Spider offhandedly. 'Two lively horses might be a bit much.'

Susan scarcely heard. Where were the tricks the big stallion tried on just about everyone? He was inventive too, mixing them up, adding a few more. His black coat gleamed like satin and he was moving as though he had every confidence in his rider.

'You look disappointed, Miss Drummond,' Thorn Sinclair called to her. 'Waiting for me to come off?'

She gave him a bright smile. 'For heaven's sake, why? Mephisto is almost an old pensioner.'

'Feel up to riding him yourself?'

'I ride him all the time.'

'Then you must be mad. He's far too strong for a little thing like you.'

'I'm game for anything, Mr Sinclair,' she called tightly.

'Exactly, but I'd call it foolhardy.'

'Call it what you like,' she muttered, willing the unpredictable Mephisto to get in a good buck.

It just didn't happen, and as they rode off Susan was forced into calling out pleasantly: 'Enjoy yourselves!'

'Now ain't that somethin'!' Spider shook his head. 'I reckon I've seen nuthin' short of a miracle. He ain't no novice, that's for sure. I sure hope you knew that, girlie, before you set him up.'

'I didn't set him up,' Susan protested.

'Yep, ya did,' Spider nodded solemnly. 'Gets ya goat, does he, Susy?'

'He does a bit.' Susan kept her eyes on the riding figures in the distance. 'Anyway, he told me he played polo, so he's used to a bit of rough-house. For all I know, he could be a close relative of Sinclair Hill. It just occurred to me that they share a name.'

'Sure reminds me of someone,' Spider added amazingly.

'Really?' Susan couldn't have been more surprised. 'Who?'

'Dunno. Someone.' Spider screwed up his eyes. 'Someone that's been on this property some time.'

'In that case I'd know him.'

'I've been around a lot longer than you, Susy.' Spider was still pondering. 'It could evena been ya granddad's time.'

'You mean he's a reincarnation?'

'Don't know nuthin' about his religion,' Spider shook out some tobacco, 'but I've certainly seen him some place. Just how and when I can't say.'

'Well, think on it, Spider, won't you?'

'Sure knows his way around horses. Got the kinda voice they like.'

Women too! Susan thought waspishly.

It was her job to see that the guests were being kept happily occupied, so she found herself during the course of the morning, sharing a canoe with the children, taking an unscheduled dip and organising riding lessons for the afternoon. One way and another it was a tiring day, but at least she had the satisfaction of knowing the children were having a glorious time. City-bred, this was their very first experience of camping and the country life, and they took to it like the ducks on the large pond. Lady, her own beloved Shetland pony, had never been so fêted and she was, of course, perfect for the riding lessons.

She and Spider with the excited help of the children were just finishing off feeding the string of horses when Geoff Munro, Patricia's long-time suitor, arrived.

'Hello there, Geoff!' Susan went towards him, smoothing her hay-filled hair.

'Susan,' he greeted her pleasantly. 'Patricia at home?'

'Well, she's on the property somewhere,' Susan told him brightly, 'showing one of our guests something of the countryside.'

Astonishment quickly followed Geoff's initial expression of disappointment. '*Patricia* is?'

'I'll admit it does seem strange.'

Geoff shrugged and smiled at her rather hesitantly. 'It's so absolutely beautiful here I expect she's just out enjoying the day. Who is it? I suppose a girl around her age?'

'If I were to tell you a tall, dark, impressive stranger, what would you say?'

'I'd say you were pulling my leg.' Fair, conventionally good-looking and always tranquil-looking, Geoff now managed to look smug.

'Not only that he's revoltingly rich!'

'You're a prankster, I know.' Geoff grinned at her quite cheerfully. 'I thought we might go out for dinner—take a run down to Surfers Paradise or into Brisbane. Only take us an hour or so. We'll go in my car.'

'Are you inviting *me*?' Susan asked humorously.

'Well, of course you're very welcome.' Geoff looked embarrassed.

'There's no danger of that. I was only fooling.' Susan looked down at her hands that were work-worn to a rather distressing degree. 'How's the family?' she asked briskly. 'Business?'

'Both fine.' Geoff's white, easy smile soon disposed of that. 'You know, Susan, I don't like to hurt your feelings, but don't you think the house is getting just the tiniest air of neglect? It's so very handsome, I don't like to see it.'

Susan was faintly angry, but she tried to keep herself unmoved. A lot of the time she thought Geoff a perfect ass. 'Perhaps you'd like to come over with a tin of paint?'

'Forgive me, sweetie, I have no aptitude for that sort of thing.'

'Neither has Patricia.'

While they were walking, Geoff was continuing his highly critical inspection. 'Surely it's occurred to you, Susan, you can't keep this up.'

'Please, Geoff, there's no point in discussing it.' What business was it really of Geoff's?

He told her. 'You'll have to get around to it some time.' He put his arm around her shoulder and hugged her. 'Strangely enough, Mum and Dad think you're marvellous?.

'But you don't.'

'I have to think of Patricia. I can understand your feelings, of course, but then, naturally, I don't like seeing Patricia distressed and unhappy.'

Susan came to a dead halt and looked up at him. 'Sometimes I think Paddy would be dis-satisfied with Paradise. She's my sister and I love her, but ask yourself, Geoff, isn't she just that least bit pampered?'

'I wouldn't dream of her being anything else.' Geoff said loyally.

'You might if you were married. I know you come from a very comfortable sort of home, but your mother is a highly accomplished housewife. She keeps the place beautifully, running smoothly, she looks after you and your father, she's a great cook and she manages to fit in some spectacular gardening and lots of outside activities. You mightn't be thinking about it now, but your mother is going to be a hard act to follow.'

'I love Patricia,' Geoff said doggedly. 'I've always loved her and I guess I always will.'

'It's kinda romantic!' Susan gave him a wry glance. 'Well, *vive l'amour*. The question is, who's going to get up and cook breakfast? Or are you planning on going without? Learning to cook has never been one of Paddy's considerations.'

'It doesn't matter,' Geoff maintained a shade unhappily. 'Call it what you like—obsession, for want of a better word. Patricia has always been my dream girl.'

'Well, good luck to you!' Susan turned on him her green, lustrous gaze. 'Who is to say who's suitable for anyone else anyway?'

Geoff smiled at her and glanced away in the distance. 'You're a good kid, Susy. You always were. I might as well go look for Patricia. Which direction did they take?'

'Well, to tell you the truth I don't really know.'

'Those kids are making an awful din, aren't they?' Geoff looked rather disapprovingly towards the sparkling wide reach of the creek.

'This is their first time camping. They're having a wonderful time.'

'What a way to make money!' Geoff muttered.

'Don't tell me it's a good idea,' Susan returned ironically.

'I rather thought, from what Patricia tells me, that your mother is becoming increasingly upset at having strangers in the house.'

'Not this weekend, Geoff.' Susan patted his arm. 'Both she and Paddy are having a lovely time. You weren't really listening before when I told you we're entertaining a true aristocrat. A man my mother and sister delight to communicate with.'

'A *man*? Gracious!'

'Patricia has been with him since early morning.' There, that should liven things up!

'Your mother wouldn't allow it!' Geoff exclaimed.

'He has a Ferrari parked in our garage. What luxury! He might even agree to chauffeur you out to dinner.'

'You're kidding me, of course.'

'Would I kid you about Patricia? Geoff, my boy, your girl is being stolen right from out under your nose.'

'Damn it,' Geoff replied helplessly. 'Damn it!'

'Not enough, Geoff. You should charge out to find her.' Susan glanced over the rolling downs suffused with the mellow, golden brilliance of late afternoon. 'On second thoughts you don't have to. Here they come.'

With a muffled exclamation, Geoff spun around. 'I say,' he muttered. 'I say!'

'Tall, isn't he?' Susan's eyes narrowed over the approaching figures. 'Paddy looks as if she's having a bit of difficulty keeping up with his stride.'

'She's not waving!' Geoff cried hoarsely.

'Perhaps she hasn't seen you yet.'

'Who *is* he?' Geoff managed finally, while the two figures found their way down the grassy, sun-dappled undulations; Patricia's blonde slenderness and the tall, lean, powerfully built figure.

'They look a picture, don't they?' remarked Susan.

'Damned if I know,' Geoff said violently. 'You haven't told me—what's his name?'

'Sinclair,' Susan answered brightly. 'Thorn Sinclair.'

'Sinclair! My God, that's the last straw!'

'You know him?' Susan about-faced.

'Sweetie, you don't know a damn thing outside your own little world. Thorn Sinclair, if the reports of him are true and that really *is* Sinclair, is some kind of millionaire financier. Hell, there was a whole article on him in the *Bulletin* the other day. It read almost like a movie. Born with a silver spoon in his mouth, very well connected, father a big businessman, lost heavily in that Golden Reef junket, maternal grandfather Sir Ian Thornton who held a number of important diplomatic posts and owned a string of racehorses . . .'

'Don't tell me,' Susan said faintly. 'It could not be, but it is. Prince Supreme was bred on Cobalt Downs. It won the Melbourne Cup for Sir Ian Thornton and even more importantly, for Grandpa. He used to say it was the sweetest success of his life.'

'So what's he doing here?' Geoff asked belligerently. 'A man like that is forever hatching some scheme.'

'Well, I'm certainly not giving him any encouragment.' Susan took a deep breath. 'I feel a fool.'

'Why?'

'I absolutely am. Grandpa took us all to

Melbourne to see the Prince running. I met Sir Ian at the time. I was only a little girl, but I remember the aura he had, like Grandpa, the way he shook my hand. He was a big man too, and as I go right back his grandson has a decided look of him. Probably that's what was fazing Spider. Paddy and I were at school, but Sir Ian did travel to Cobalt Downs with his trainer.' They were closer now and Patricia's loosened blonde hair was blowing forward on her cheeks.

'This is unbelievable,' Geoff said with hostility. 'I see disaster in this man coming here.'

'Hello Susan ... Geoff!' Patricia called in her clear, sweet voice.

Susan lifted her hand and wiggled her fingers, but Geoff stood his ground stony-faced.

'Don't see trouble, Geoff, before there is any,' Susan warned.

'Patricia looks radiant.'

'Healthy exercise and all that.'

'Seriously, Susan,' Geoff whispered urgently. 'You always know the one that's different.'

Unconsciously Susan's hand went to her tousled curls, then as she realised she was trying to make herself look more presentable, she dropped her hand. Let Patricia look like a daffodil in her filmy yellow dress. It was hard to look stylish when you had to pull yourself out of the creek.

'Why, look who's here! Hello, Geoff,' Patricia cried delightedly, and with a quick little Southern belle giggle introduced the two men.

'Munro,' Thorn Sinclair acknowledged the younger man rather drily, and shook his hand.

'I'm very pleased to meet you, Mr Sinclair,' Geoff announced with a mixture of hypocrisy and triumph. 'I was just telling Susan here I'd read a whole feature on you the other day.'

'I must try and get a copy,' said Susan.

'You haven't told *me* anything about this,' Patricia turned to him accusingly.

'To be quite honest, I didn't read the damned thing.'

'Please do be quite honest,' Susan invited pointedly.

'About what, Miss Drummond?'

It seemed to her his silver eyes narrowed dangerously. 'Why didn't you mention that you were Sir Ian Thornton's grandson?'

'I'm a fanatic on not talking family.'

'I don't think I'm getting this,' said Patricia. 'You mean you're related to the man who bought Prince Supreme? The man who won the Melbourne Cup?'

'People always say that.' The golden slanting sun gave his skin a look of polished bronze. ' "Not Sir Ian Thornton, the distinguished diplomat. The man who won the Melbourne Cup.' "

'You don't understand the honour?'

'My dear Miss Drummond, I'm as horsey as you are.'

'Wonderful. A wonderful horseman,' Patricia said hastily. 'I've never seen Mephisto so beautifully behaved, not even for you, Susan.'

'He's too strong for you,' Thorn Sinclair told Susan again, compelling her to meet his gaze.

'My father bought him. I keep him,' she said. 'Anyway I know all his tricks. He seldom tries them out on me.'

'And when he does?'

'We have a mild tussle. Why are you worrying about me, Mr Sinclair?'

'Wouldn't one worry about a baby given a dangerous toy?'

'Not Susan,' Patricia said contentedly. 'She's enormously competent—Daddy saw to that.'

'And what did he expect of you?' Thorn Sinclair asked her gravely.

'Oh, to look pretty,' Patricia laughed. 'He often used to say I was the positive image of Mummy when he met and fell in love with her.'

'None of them dreamed there would be a gipsy in the family,' said Susan. 'Listen, I have to run along. See you, Geoff.'

'Yes, goodbye, Susan,' Geoff responded with colour in his cheeks. 'I wonder if I might have a word with you, Patricia?'

'What now, Geoff?' Patricia asked with faint impatience.

'I thought we might take a run to Surfers, or something. Have dinner. There are still a few restaurants we haven't worked our way through.'

'What about the Jade Room?' Thorn Sinclair suggested helpfully. 'The seafood especially is superb.'

'I don't think I'm in the mood to go out tonight,' Patricia explained.

'Oh, *do* come, Patricia.' Geoff, as always, was reduced to begging. 'I love to see you dressed up.'

'All right, then,' Patricia laughed gaily. 'What about if we all go?'

'Brilliant!' said Susan. 'I get up at five o'clock.' Not to speak of having no dress.

'I'll leave you young people to make up your minds.' Thorn Sinclair walked off towards Susan. 'Nice to meet you, Munro.'

'I'll remember to show Susan that article,' he said.

'And *me*.' Patricia gave the impression that she was torn two ways.

'So what are you going to do now?' Thorn Sinclair asked Susan suavely. 'Chop the wood?'

'I know how to swing an axe.'

'As a weapon, or what?'

'You're really too sharp for me,' she said acidly.

'I don't know so much about that. Where are we hurrying to, by the way?'

'I've got a few jobs to do before nightfall.'

'If you like, I'll help you.'

'No.'

'That wasn't very polite.' He glanced down on her, unsmilingly.

'As it happens, I suspected your motives for coming here the very moment I laid eyes on you,' Susan told him.

'And what *are* my motives, little Miss Drummond?'

'I daresay you have some multi-million-dollar scheme roughly worked out in your mind. This is only part of the strategy.'

'And I'm going to put it to you to be my partner?'

'I'm not interested.'

'Even when I can help you?'

'How?' She stopped quickly, wheeling to face him. 'Can you help me keep my home?'

'I hadn't considered that up until now.' He looked down at her, flushed cheeks and darkened emerald eyes.

'You mean you want to move us out? Take over the valley?'

'I don't think so.' He was studying her rather sombrely. 'You're much too gallant. I always salute a thoroughbred's courage.'

'But you had something in mind?' She had come nearer, staring up into his face.

'I've always got something in mind,' he said evasively. 'What if I loaned you the money to make a go of this place?'

'Are you serious?' she looked at him doubtfully.

'I am now.'

'But *why*?'

'It's not such a bad idea.' His silver eyes glinted humorously.

'A little idea. Don't you specialise in the big ones?'

'I can see exactly why a big idea would hurt you. Can you imagine me literally dragging you out of your home?'

'At least you understand.' Susan started walking again, a petite figure in her tight jeans and skimpy shirt.

'A bit rough on your mother and Patricia, though, isn't it? I gather over these weekends emotions run high.'

'Ah, here it comes,' she accused him. 'The hard sell.'

'Do you think that's what it is?' Thorn put his hand on her shoulder and turned her towards him.

'Sounds like it.' Characteristically she tilted her chin.

'But it isn't. I gather your father left you all the clout?'

'He knew I was the only one who cared like he did.'

'He didn't worry that the load would be too heavy for these shoulders?' Now he held her by both hands.

'Mr Drummond,' she said angrily, 'I'm a lot tougher than I look.'

'Because you've got your hands like a gardener's boy?'

'I *am* a gardener,' she said sharply. 'I want to turn the sprinkler on the vegetable garden, if you'll let me. Don't forget you praised these very same vegetables last night.'

'So you're going to kill yourself trying to hold on to your heritage?'

'Not at all,' she said sarcastically. 'You're going to give me a loan.'

'You'd take it?' He walked around to the tap and turned it on.

'No. I've a feeling there would be too many strings.'

'Explain yourself, Miss Drummond.' He found his way back to her. 'You can't think I have a personal interest in you?'

'For a moment there last night I thought you had.'

'Forget that, little one. I'd like to make it quite clear, I don't seduce teenagers.'

'I'm twenty,' she said coldly.

'Okay, you're twenty. Are you giving me the all-clear?'

'Indeed I'm not! I'm a good and virtuous girl.'

'With a dollop of seductress thrown in.'

The sprinkler started to play up and she gave an exasperated little moan. 'Does *nothing* around here work?'

'Things do wear out with the passage of time.' Thorn backtracked to the tap, made a few adjustments and the water began to play again over the highly productive kitchen garden. 'You really need a much more efficient system.'

'Are you offering to take responsibility for that?' she asked lightly, looking with pleasure at her beautiful salad crop.

'Why don't you let me think about it?' He sat on the stone garden seat away from the spray and pulled her down beside him. 'Don't tell me you're the gardener?'

'Just look at my hands!' She held them palms up with a wry expression.

'Don't you think you ought to wear gloves?' He took the hand nearest him, smoothing his thumb into the cupped palm.

'I daresay, but they're not always handy.' Her heartbeat had picked up with indecent haste, curious little flutterings all over her body.

'No, sit there,' he said drily, 'I want to talk to you.'

'Then you'd better give me back my hand.'

'Do you put cream on them, or what?'

'Occasionally. Listen,' she said, quickly flushing, 'I know most women probably find you fantastic, but I've got to run.'

'All right. No need.' He gave her her hand back. 'Have you any rich suitors, by the way?'

'Unhappily, no. Paddy has,' she added brightly. 'Geoff's people are well heeled and Geoff as their only offspring stands to get everything.'

'But she's not in love with him?'

'He isn't exciting enough, as you know very well.'

'But he's in love with her?'

'Beyond question. It's rather beautiful really. Clearly you've upset him.'

'My dear child, how?' He glanced down at her piquant profile, rounded forehead, delicately retroussé nose, full, moulded mouth, determined chin; a quite different profile from her sister's very regular, classic features.

'Patricia isn't in the habit of going walkabout with perfect strangers.'

'She's a very charming young woman.'

'I don't trust you,' Susan said. 'Neither does Geoff.'

'Patricia does,' he jeered softly.

'It wouldn't occur to her that you're not a gentleman.'

'Insulting little devil, aren't you?' He gave one of her glossy curls a not-too-friendly tug.

'It seems to me I'm responsible for the well-being of my family.'

'All the same, little one, one gets the feeling the job is too big for you. All I can say at this stage is, I'm prepared to help you out with a loan if you'll allow me to tell you exactly what you need.'

'But why?' Susan was so deep in perplexity she spoke fiercely.

'I don't even know myself.'

'You didn't come here to say that?' she accused him.

'No.' His startling, light eyes were moving all over her face. 'I came here to buy your half of the valley. I own the rest.'

'*You* do? You can't. It belongs to some big corporation. They're going to turn it into a multi-million-dollar sporting complex or something.'

'In fact, I hope, one of the greatest golf courses in the country and a home for polo. If you mixed a bit more, you'd have heard the plans have finally been laid.'

'And you're behind it?'

'Why are you so stunned?' he queried.

'I can't believe it, that's why. Patricia probably thinks you find her attractive and all you're after is Cobalt Downs.'

'Maybe I was,' he said harshly, 'and I *do* find Patricia attractive. That's why your being her sister is so bizarre.'

'Of course I'll never sell to you.'

'Of course not,' his voice was now mild. 'Clearly it would kill you.'

Susan thought she dragged herself up, when actually she moved swiftly. 'It must be dreadful having to con people.'

As she turned to fling a green-eyed glance at him she saw the dark anger move through him. '*No*,' she murmured with some bravado edged with panic.

'My word, yes!' His silvery eyes were blazing. 'Who's conning you, you little brat? For reasons I can't even explain to myself, I'd like to help you.'

'Softening me up?'

'Don't say you didn't ask for it.'

From the very first second she had laid eyes on him things had got out of control. She couldn't run through the sprinkler, so she tore around the side of the house like an explosive child with an irate parent in pursuit.

Thorn caught her by the large pond, lifting her high in his arms. 'What you need, little Miss Drummond, is to cool off.'

'I'll take you with me,' she warned.

'Go tell it to the ducks!'

Who was going to help her? no one.

'You *brute*!' she exclaimed.

Thorn wasn't even listening. Though she tried and tried to pull him with her by tightening her stranglehold on his neck he actually threw her out into the water with all the lightning ease of a flying stone.

She landed with a splash and came up thrashing wildly in her anger. 'I can't *stand* brutes and bullies!' she gasped.

'And I don't admire insolent little girls.'

'How dare you!' She had to swim out, then scramble through the emerald green reeds. 'Don't think for one minute you're going to get dinner tonight!'

'There now!' he began to speak to her like a fractious filly. 'Give me your hand.'

'I might as well,' she groaned defeatedly, and when their fingers locked let him see her wildly rebellious face.

They went back together, Thorn losing his footing on the slippery grass. 'You little brat!'

'Did I hurt you?' Suddenly she was laughing, her small face radiant. He was so damned certain of himself, she had yearned to bring him down. Literally.

They were almost in the water, half hidden by the whispering, green grass, decorated here and there with clumps of wild iris. Then, as suddenly as they had been lying side by side, he half pinned her slender body under his own. 'You can't start a war without expecting reprisals,' he warned.

'Just you let me up!' The excitement that was leaping up in her she fended off with aggression.

'Well, I never!' He glanced down at her soaked body. 'You're not wearing a damned thing under that shirt!'

In fact, a button had gone missing and it was almost open to her waist. '*Let me go*,' she said rigidly, her colour flaring.

'You're staying exactly where you are. They mightn't discover us for a week.'

'*Please.*' Susan licked away the pond water with the tip of her tongue.

'I see. Now you're going to play the helpless little female?' His expression was disturbing, wary, amused, and not quite in control. 'You're very unusual, Miss Drummond.'

'And you're a. . .'

'I'm nothing of the kind.' He stared into her agitated eyes. 'What's the matter with you? You act the little devil, then when you drive me to action, you start to panic. If I put my hand over your heart I'd find it fluttering like a bird.'

'If I don't get out of these wet clothes,' she said excitedly, 'I might run a temperature.' In fact she never caught cold.

'The trouble is, you're half out of them now.'

'And you shouldn't be looking.' All of a sudden

her voice wavered, born of a general upset. Her hair was sprinkled with diamonds of moisture and her large green eyes were filled with uncertainty and the fear of involvement beyond her slight experience.

'No, I shouldn't,' Thorn actually said. From abruptness and a hard, masculine strength he was as gentle as a sensitive, caring big brother. 'Don't forget to sew that button on tonight.'

She was upright, wet to the skin and a little tearful. 'I'm afraid you've got grass stains on your clothes.'

'Which hasn't happened to me since I was about fourteen.' He glanced down indifferently at his expensively clad body. 'Shall I sling you over my shoulder and carry you up to the house?'

'Let me find my own way, *please*.'

'All right, Susan,' he gave her a sharp, very disturbing smile. 'You're not the best behaved landlady I've ever met in my life.'

'And heaven knows, you're just as disagreeable a guest!'

CHAPTER FOUR

'I really think he's interested in Patricia, don't you?' Julia Drummond turned on her younger daughter a quietly triumphant face.

'I have no idea, Mamma.' Susan swept her wide-brimmed hat off her head and collapsed into the planter's chair.

'You're not sulking, are you, Susan?' her mother asked her sharply.

'Whatever for?' Susan felt furiously hurt and affronted. 'You've no idea how tiring it is, Mamma, running around after the guests.'

'I told you you shouldn't bring those children up to the house. They paid to stay in the *grounds*.'

'I only took them up to the tower. They were fascinated when I told them it was once used to spot any hostile blacks. A lot of squatters were driven out by the relentless raiding of the Aborigines. At least the Drummonds were smart and humane enough to establish friendly relations and employ them on the station. Not all the white settlers treated the Aborigines half so well.'

'We're not talking about ancient history,' Julia said shortly. 'We're talking about your sister. With none of our old standing I've been making myself ill worrying about what's going to happen to her. She's so lovely, so sweet-natured, she deserves a prince.'

'When the indications are that Mr Sinclair is a bit of a devil!'

'Now what on earth does *that* mean?' Julia gave her daughter a black look. 'It's as obvious as it could be, Mr Sinclair is a gentleman and an extraordinarily attractive man. Of course he's older, but all to the good. He's established and fairly obviously wealthy. Patricia could take her place at the side of a man like that. He could keep her in style.'

'He'd have to employ a lot of servants. Paddy's actually never done a tap of work in her life.'

'And what have *you* done, Susan?' her mother asked her. 'Don't feel smug about opening up our home to a lot of strangers!'

'It was the only way, Mamma,' Susan protested. 'I can't believe you would want to sell our home. The Drummonds and the McKenzies were the first settlers in this valley.'

'And the McKenzies have gone.'

'There was only old Miss McKenzie left, and she held out as long as she possibly could. The valley is enchanted—Grandpa used to say that. I'd do anything rather than sell it.'

'I hear Miss McKenzie was paid a fortune,' said her mother.

'And then they picked up a bargain,' Susan said harshly. 'Somehow I hate to think of her dying in a home. She was used to a very different way of life.'

'I know,' Julia agreed. 'But then she was much too frail to be left by herself. No one could ever find out exactly who bought the place.'

'That damned valley resort crowd,' Susan said angrily. 'Next thing we'll have hairy-legged golfers and all the racy polo crowd filling up the valley— probably landing in helicopters. We'll have lots of company then.'

'Really, when one thinks about it,' said Julia, 'we could probably get three times as much as Catriona. She merely *had* to sell out. We could sit still and bargain.'

'And then where would we go?' Susan asked bleakly.

'Forgive me, my dear, but you can't expect me to think exclusively of you. So you're profoundly attached to the place, so am I, but I have Patricia to think of. Peter as well. You do know you're keeping us all poor for a dream?'

'We're not poor, Mamma,' Susan sighed. 'Compared to ordinary people we're still considered to be the élite. For all you say we've lost our old standing, you're still Mrs Drummond of Cobalt Downs and we're still highly eligible young ladies. You can't beat prime real estate for a dowry.'

'Except you won't release it.'

'Do you really want me to, Mummy?' Susan asked dispiritedly.

'I think I'll see how Patricia's friendship with Mr Sinclair progresses. Honestly, he never took his eyes off her at dinner last night, and poor Geoff became increasingly unhappy. He's a good boy and I suppose a good catch, but a man like Thorn Sinclair made him appear very countrified and callow.'

'Yes, it *was* rather dreadful for Geoff.' Susan gave a frowning stare into the shimmering distance. Faced with the prospect of losing Thorn Sinclair's company for the evening, Patricia had duly informed Geoff that she would much rather stay home, and of course he was invited to dinner. It had not been a happy evening for him, though admittedly a lot of it had been his own fault. Geoff had come down from university with a very good law degree, yet he had sat at the dinner table in an awkward, undistinguished near silence but with the faintly agonised expression of someone who was doing a lot of urgent private thinking.

Susan supposed he had to. Patricia's bright, lovely face mirrored exactly her pleasure in Thorn Sinclair's company. He was certainly very articulate and skilful at bringing people out. The Ashtons had chatted happily about foreign places, the art galleries they had visited all around the world, Julia had spoken of their own art collection without boasting, Patricia had shone with happiness. Only she and Geoff were kept from thoroughly enjoying the conversation, for one reason or the other. Even this morning they had gone off together, for a stroll after breakfast, then a ride into the hill country. He had to be, Susan thought bleakly, the most devious of men. Sir Ian Thornton's grandson, a millionaire entrepreneur, a fascinator of sheltered girls. She detested the thought of his hurting Patricia. She could be falling in love with him, for instance. It wasn't a very reassuring thought. Susan had the certain feeling there had been many women in Thorn Sinclair's life; beautiful, experienced women who had shared his bed as well as his conversation. She and Patricia had been reared as strictly as two Victorian maidens, and maidens they still were, albeit of an age to be seduced. With Thorn Sinclair it just had to be Experience.

'Do you know, Susan, I've spoken to you three times,' Julia was saying to her crossly.

'I'm sorry, Mamma, I was thinking.'

'What about?'

'Paddy and Thorn Sinclair.'

'You feel resentment because they're together?'

'No, Mamma, not for a second.' Susan shook her gleaming head. 'I just think it would be a mistake for either you or Paddy to get your hopes up. He's obviously a man who's lived—that's to say, I suppose he's got a long history of love affairs. Why isn't he married? He's so terribly the kind of man women hanker after it seems a little bit strange. Perhaps he was married a couple of times, divorced?'

Her mother sat up very straight. 'You can't be serious, Susan! Mr Sinclair described himself as a bachelor.'

'I suppose you *are* if you haven't got a present wife.'

'You must be very jealous of Patricia, I think,' her mother suggested nastily.

'No, Mamma—I love her very much. I don't want to see her hurt. Paddy takes things to heart. Remember how upset she was when Brett Casey didn't fall in love with her?'

'You were at fault there, Susan, as I remember.' Julia's blue eyes glittered. 'You went after him yourself.'

'What nonsense!'

'Please drop the subject, Susan.' Julia stood up. 'I hope you're not going to make any more promises to those children. They're well behaved, I'll admit, but really, dear, I'd like to keep them out. Try to remember this is *my* home.'

'What's the matter with you today?' Annie later enquired.

'Worries. Problems.' Susan watched Annie expertly throw together the ingredients for a cheese and spinach pie. 'Mamma really hates what I'm doing, doesn't she?'

'Terribly vulgar!' Annie's feelings got the better of her and she mimicked Julia's cultured tones.

'The only alternative then is to sell. It's the last thing I want, but I seem to be the only one who wants to hold on to what the Drummonds fought for.'

'I told you, love,' Annie's comfortable face

looked drawn, 'it's nearly impossible without the help of your mother. Even if she doesn't help us physically, knowing she approves of what we're doing would make it so much easier and set your mind at rest. As it is, it seems hopeless. Here we are on a fine morning in the kitchen while your sister is out riding and you're constantly in a state of apology for bringing in our main source of income. It seems crazy!'

'Maybe I'm the crazy one,' Susan sighed. 'Maybe I'm fighting a losing battle. If we sell up we'll all be very comfortably off, and this is obviously what Mamma and Paddy want. Peter backs me. He wants the money, of course, but he knows what holding on to the property means to me. Why doesn't everyone think it's as beautiful as I do? Why doesn't everyone look at a tree and say Great-Grandpa planted that, or see that stand of gums? Grandma Alice planted those when the men went off to the war. It's all part of us, something felt deeply in the blood.'

'You're not most people, Susy.' Annie looked up to study the girl's beloved face. There were tears in her eyes, though she blinked them furiously away. 'You're either like that, or you're not. Unfortunately for you, the rest of your family don't share your sense of heritage, or your love for the land. You can't blame them, that's the way they are.'

'But it's going to force us out of here, Annie!'

'I know.' Annie slapped the pastry more vigorously than she intended. 'You feel betrayed, don't you?'

'I feel I'll be breaking my word to Daddy. He knew that when the time came I would be the only one to try and hang on to Cobalt Downs.'

'Even if you put yourself in a position of near-slavery. The work's too heavy for you, love.' Annie's voice was gentle. 'Do you know, you're only bone, and if they weren't such good bones you'd be scrawny!'

'I was thinking the same thing myself.' Susan looked down at her outstretched arms. 'Give me a glass of milk!'

The weekend passed with a barbecue for Sunday's lunch for the campers, and Susan, pressed into staying, decided to do so. No one really needed her at the house. Annie could look after the lunch and her mother and Patricia were more than capable of keeping their guests very happily entertained. So she stayed.

'We've had the most wonderful time!' the children told her with bright eyes. 'We've been hoping it would never end, but of course we have to go back tonight. School in the morning.'

'One thing you can be very sure of, Miss Drummond,' Bob Irving added with enthusiasm, 'we'll be back again.'

'Lovely!' For once Susan sat back and relaxed while the children waited on her hand and foot.

'You wouldn't care to sell your Shetland pony, would you?' Mrs Irving asked her. 'The children adore her.'

'*I* do, even more.'

'I thought so, dear,' Mrs Irving laughed. 'Here, have some more salad. You're one girl who has the space for it. Why, you must have a twenty-inch waist.'

'So did you,' her husband called to her. 'Once upon a time!'

They were such pleasant people and so genuinely appreciative of such a beautiful property, Susan was sorry to see them leave. She and Spider stood waving as they all departed. Both families had in fact become friendly; children and adults and the Masons made a point of telling Susan they would tell all their friends where they could enjoy a blissful weekend's camping.

'Damn sorry to see them go,' said Spider with a pleased expression. 'I reckon those kids are gunna drive their parents mad to get a pony of their own.'

'All children should have a pony,' said Susan. 'Thanks for the way you were so nice to them, Spider. Over and above the call of duty.'

'Ya know I'll do anythin' to help you out, Susy. Anyway, they were nice kids, treated the cows like people. I reckon they've never seen a cow milked in their lives. Not a one of them that didn't tell me they were gunna come back.'

'If we're still here,' Susan murmured.

'You'll be here, Susy,' Spider muttered fiercely. 'Why don't ya fascinate all six foot three of that Mr Sinclair?'

'Paddy's doing that,' Susan laughed.

'I don't think he listens to a word she says.'

'Heavens!' Susan turned to her offsider with rounded eyes. 'That's not very gallant.'

'Ya know what I mean. She's nice little girl, Miss Patricia, and I reckon he reconnises that, but she ain't exactly 'is cup o' tea.'

'And *I* am?' Susan's small face was wreathed in smiles. 'Did I tell you he threw me into the pond?'

'Eh?' Spider looked decidedly nonplussed. 'What for?' he asked blankly.

'For giving cheek.'

'When ya the mistress here?'

'Mamma's the mistress, Spider. No, I just accused Mr Sinclair of being a con man.'

'Ya didn't!' Spider was so dismayed his voice went hoarse. 'I hope ya didn't say that, Susy.'

'I did. What's more, you'll never guess who he is.'

'Tell me.' Spider fixed her with a fuzzy stare.

'Sir Ian Thornton's grandson.'

'My gawd!'

'Though you'd be surprised.' Parrots flew over their heads like coloured flowers and Susan looked after them. 'Not only that, I'm fairly certain he or his syndicate bought the McKenzie place and his original plan was to try and buy here.'

'Struth!' Spider collapsed on to a hollow log. 'Then he's some kind of big-time developer?'

'You might say that. I believe he and his partners are going to turn the valley into a kind of highland resort—a world class golf course, tennis, squash, horse riding, the works, I imagine, and of course polo. Can't you just see him thundering down the field with everyone else backing off so he can have a full, free swing?'

'Powerful-lookin' bloke,' Spider agreed. 'Come to that, so was Thornton. It seems to be a big plus in a man's favour.'

'Especially when they can just pick you up and throw you out into midstream.'

'So what 'appened?' Spider looked shaken.

'Nothing much. I called him a brute and a bully and when he tried to make amends and help me out I pulled him back with me. Not far enough, unfortunately, but it was a priceless moment.'

'*Susy!*' Spider muttered, and started to scratch his head. 'That's not the way to a man's 'eart.'

'I'm certain he hasn't got one.' Susan sat down beside Spider on the log. 'But he's very smooth. He offered to help us out.'

' 'Ow?' Spider merely grunted.

'With a loan.'

'A *loan*?'

Susan nodded. 'He thinks we have a very nice little idea and he'd be pleased to chip in.'

'What for?'

'I think you know the answer, Spider, my friend. To soften me up. Little girls can't really make a success of anything. One needs a big, powerful man. When I crash he can always say he gave me my chance, then he can sit down and work out a deal. You can be absolutely sure Mamma and Paddy will meet him at the conference table.'

'Perhaps he just a decent bloke?' Spider ventured. 'I kinda like him. He looks right atcha when he's talkin' to ya, and not down his nose either. I reckon a real classy bloke is always polite. Like his granddad. Life's full of those bloody snobs.'

'It is indeed.' Susan smiled ironically. 'Did you notice a whole section of fencing has come down along the West Fork?'

'I surely did. I'll get on to it tomorrow, but I'll need some things from the town.'

'Then we'll go in,' Susan decided. 'I have the Irvings' and the Masons' cheques in my pocket. The Ashtons' will be a lot more and our Mr Sinclair has been drinking our best wine.'

'It's not enough Susy, ya know that.'

'Not you, Spider. That's too much.'

'Facts is facts, Susy.' Spider gave her a glance strongly laced with sympathy. 'Why don't ya have another chat with Mr Sinclair?'

'When he wants to take us over?' Alarm bells rang in Susan's brain. 'That's what brought him here in the first place, not the country weekend interest. He's just plain looking us over.'

'An' I can't help thinkin', Susy, he likes what he sees.'

It was dusk when Susan found her way back to
the house, but instead of going straight in, she
took refuge in the garden watching the last of the
mysterious, mauve light. At this time of day the
peace and quiet of the place was remarkable: apart
from the calls of the birds nearly all the sounds
were made by the wind. It sighed through the grass
and rustled the leaves of the trees and the shrubs.
The delicious scent of boronia was borne to her,
and she moved over to their old swing and sat in
it, touching her feet to the ground so it began to
move gently.

'Higher, Daddy, *higher*! I want to *fly*!'

The eerie sound of her own voice came back to
her caught and held through the years. She had
always been the one who had wanted to do
something daring—ride the tearaway horses,
explore the rough and tumble sections of the creek,
go along with the men on their muster. She
supposed she had been a tomboy child, without
Patricia's ladylike and sometimes fluttery habits
and Peter's ambition, settling very early in life on
being a doctor. But she and her father had been
such friends. Common interests and an intense
love of their own world had bound them closely
together. Her father, too, had always been
extremely pressed. Grandpa, although extremely
reduced in his private fortune, had nevertheless
spent extravagantly right up until his final, fatal
stroke. After that there were death duties and
creditors and some of the worst years for the beef
industry. But her father had been determined to
hold onto his birthright. As she was now.

She could feel her eyes filling with tears. If she
bowed to all the pressures Patricia would have her
wardrobe full of beautiful, expensive clothes. Her
mother would buy a smart house, probably in her

favourite city, Melbourne, and they would lead a
life more suited to their temperaments. For all
that, perhaps they did deserve better. It was a very
quiet life now at Cobalt Downs. They never
entertained, never enjoyed the frequent trips to the
southern capitals. Once her mother had bought
everything in sight with no clear idea as to how it
was going to get paid. And her father had allowed
it, beggaring himself so his wife could be happy.

'Susan?'

She heard an unmistakable voice call her name,
but she didn't bother to answer. Such was her
mood. Let Paddy be beautiful and amusing, she
had too many worries on her mind. Susan
launched herself into the air, but the creaking
chains gave her sheltered nook away.

'Having fun?' he called up to her with quite
unmistakable amusement.

For answer she swung higher, her slight girl's
figure outlined against the lavender sky. She
couldn't come down in any case. With his hawk-
eyed vision Thorn would notice she had been
crying.

'Susan?' There was a touch of anxiety in that
impossibly self-assured voice.

'It's all right,' she called to him. 'Therapy for my
manic-depressive mood.'

'Not so high, then,' he said sharply. 'The whole
thing is too rusty.'

'How sweet! Are you really anxious?'

'Come on down now. It's getting dark.'

'Yes, Daddy.' Her feelings were far from
daughterly. She had decided to stop in any case,
the chains were making an awful creak.

One moment she was looking towards the
ground, the next one of the chains of the old swing
gave a frightful snap and she was flung out in a

wide semicircle. *Roll*, she thought in anguish. *Roll* and you won't hurt yourself.

Over the years she had taken many spills from a horse. Once a hunter had baulked at a high fence and sent her flying over its neck at forty miles an hour. Spills were a part of life.

'A . . . a . . . ah!' She knew she had cried out.

'My goodness! Thorn looked down at her as she lay completely winded on the grass. Her small face was colourless and agonised, then her chest began to heave as she struggled for breath. 'You damn silly child!'

She would have loved to answer him, but she couldn't. Coughing and heaving and shuddering, she lay spreadeagled while the world righted itself and air came back into her lungs.

'Nothing broken, thank heavens.' He was visibly repressing much stronger language, expert hands running over her. 'Lie there. Lie quietly. Wait for things to settle.'

Her eyelids came down over her eyes, though she thought she would never forget the expression on his formidable, dark face. It was easy to see he thought her a perfect fool, that she had deliberately done something incredibly foolish. Come to think of it, it *had* been rather an awful fall.

Minutes passed while he bent over her with urgency. 'How are you now?'

'A bit vague.'

'You look like a little ghost!' he muttered.

'How can you tell, it's almost dark.'

'Stop talking. You can't be content with a word. You're into the banter.'

'So why are *you* so angry?' Susan demanded. 'I'm the one who bit the grass.'

A short distance away from them, Patricia was

running out on to the lawn. 'What's the matter?' she wanted to know.

'The swing gave way,' Thorn Sinclair answered, somewhat impatiently.

'Heavens, Susy, you weren't in the swing, were you?' Patricia knelt on the ground beside her sister.

'Just a bit of fun.' Susan tried to lift herself up on one elbow, and found herself very firmly supported.

'Why don't you stop talking!' Thorn Sinclair got a further grip on her and lifted her into his arms. 'Your voice is all husky.'

'It's better than passing out.'

'But you knew the chains were rusty.' Patricia sounded confused.

'I think I'll carry her up to her bedroom,' Thorn said. 'She was very lucky. She could have broken bones.'

Seeing the expression on Patricia's face, Susan wanted to indicate to him tactfully that he had better put her down. 'Look,' she said croakingly, 'all I need is a chair and maybe a cup of tea.'

'You look terrible!' he told her.

'Thank you!'

Patricia stared at them both with something like dismay. 'I really think she's all right, Thorn. Susan is used to lots of spills. I remember she's had some terrible ones and come up smiling.'

'She's not smiling now.'

Julia, too, was rushing out of the house. 'What on earth has happened?'

'Can't we simply forget it?' Susan muttered, but Patricia reasoned that her mother was certainly entitled to an explanation, which she gave in a funny way, half sympathetic, half accusing.

'Really, Susan, that's a funny thing for a girl of your age to be doing!'

'You're cold, Susan.' Thorn Sinclair was feeling the strange chill off her skin.

'I just feel a bit sick.' How distressing that an almost complete stranger was the only one to give her a bit of genuine sympathy.

In her room, they all stood staring down at her, but mercifully the slight feeling of nausea had passed.

'Fancy,' she said a little vaguely, 'that rather knocked me out.'

'You didn't hit your head, did you? I didn't check your head.' Thorn moved towards her and sat on the side of the bed.

'I'm sure, doctor, you'll find a lump.'

'This is no joke, Susan,' her mother snapped. 'You're always doing irresponsible things.'

'Is *that* sore?' Thorn had his long fingers speared through her hair, exploring her aching skull.

'Ouch!'

'It's not very big.'

'What a misadventure to spoil the evening,' Patricia said.

'Look, I'm sorry, but I'm perfectly all right.'

'You're getting your colour back,' Patricia observed, relieved. 'Thorn was going to take us for a run to the Coast. I'm dying to have a drive in his car.'

'You go,' Julia told them, touching Patricia's hand. 'Poor Susan, I'll have to stay with her.'

In another minute Susan thought she would scream. '*Do* stop,' she said a little tightly. 'If you were all going to go out for the evening, go. I'm no cause for concern.'

'Sure?' Patricia looked lovely and spoilt and hopeful.

'Quite sure.' Susan stood up jauntily, though she

still wasn't breathing properly. 'Nobody in their right mind would pass up a trip in a Ferrari.'

'I think I will, just this once,' Julia smiled. 'You're still rather white, Susan. I'd feel happier at home with you.'

In the morning Susan got through the chores early in preparation for her trip into the town. She might even go in and have a chat to Mr Sommerville, the bank manager. He was very much the father-figure kind of man and he had always been very courteous and helpful even when he couldn't actually lend the money.

Of all places their only guest found her collecting the eggs. 'Hi, you're up early!' she called to him over her shoulder.

'I'm always up early.' He came right up to her and began to study her as though she was a butterfly under glass. 'Feeling better?'

'Fine.'

He put out his hand and felt for the bump on the back of her head. 'It's gone down.'

'Don't be kind to me, Mr Sinclair.' Her luminous green eyes mocked him.

His rather stern expression relaxed a little. 'You're a tough little cookie, aren't you? Five feet two of fragile bones!'

'Enjoy yourself last night?' she asked pointedly.

'Very pleasant. Next time I'll take *you* out to dinner.'

'Next time?' Susan raised her black, winging brows. 'Won't you be too busy with your own life?'

'I should think I'll have to live in the valley.'

'*What?*' she gasped.

'I didn't think you'd be pleased,' Thorn said drily.

'Why would a man like you settle for the country life?'

He took the basket from her and held it after first admiring the eggs. 'My dear Miss Drummond, do you really imagine I'm going away when they're going to start laying out the course? I'm going to be in on it from the beginning. Not only is it a game I really enjoy, but I'm determined we're going to finish up with a great course. We've retained one of the best golf architects in the world and this is a fabulously beautiful and suitable valley. Just the right landscape for a fine course, a kind of natural links. It adds immeasurably to the game if the surroundings are beautiful.'

'Well, of course.' She looked up at him in some bewilderment. 'So you've got plenty of land. Why would you want Cobalt Downs?'

'Taking it off you, little one, might destroy you.'

'But why do you want it?' she persisted, shading her golden face from the sun.

'Another scheme of mine, even closer to my heart. I was a millionaire by the time I was twenty-eight. I'm thirty-four now and I'm ready to do what I really want.'

'Oh, I hope you're not going to tell me with a wife and a dozen children!'

'Well, if she feels like having them.'

'Good grief,' Susan said presently, feeling unaccountably dismayed. 'Have you already picked her out?'

'Yes, I think so. Haven't you heard of love at first sight?'

'Yes, but I wouldn't think you'd believe in it.'

'I didn't, for a long time. In any case, I'm not talking about marriage. I can easily arrange that when I want to. I'm talking about a horse empire, a stud farm where I can breed winners, the top racehorses in the country. All my business ventures are thriving and I have outstandingly qualified people to run them. A stud farm I'm going to run myself. I told you before, I'm a horse person.'

'And you were thinking of Cobalt Downs?'

'Listen, big-eyes, at one time Cobalt Downs bred some of the finest thoroughbreds in the country. You mightn't have been born into the glamour period, but you only just missed it. When my grandfather wanted a horse to win him the Melbourne Cup, he came up here to Queensland. To Cobalt Downs. I just had to see it, but when I came the first time your family were in mourning for your father. I could never have intruded.'

'But you came back to see *me*?' She felt angry and looked it.

'Actually I shelved you for quite a while. The McKenzie property was up for sale and my mind is always ticking over, seeing possibilities. The valley reminded me of certain parts of Scotland, and then I began to think about the site as a possible first-class golf course. The popularity of the game is soaring and it seemed to me I had a championship site on my hands. As it happened, my architect, Donald Scott, agrees with me. He's worked all over the world and he's very enthusiastic.'

'But you'll have people swarming all over the valley!'

'So damn it all, Susan, you can't have it all to yourself. Your era, my lady, has vanished. You call yourself a working girl, but you were brought up an aristocrat and an aristocrat you remain in your mind. All this is mine. It can only stay yours, Susan, if you can work it.'

'I'll marry a rich man!' she said hotly. 'You wouldn't know me when I'm dressed up.'

'I can imagine. You look good enough now.' Thorn looked down at her his silver eyes gleaming. 'Are you telling me you're prepared to do the Scarlett O'Hara?'

'If he's good-looking, I might.' She knew she was talking nonsense, but she didn't care.

'And if he's old and somewhat beyond making love to a young wife?'

'Who's talking about love?' she cried. 'What shall I do if I can't live here? I might just settle for a marriage of convenience, millionaires being as scarce as the jewels in a crown.'

'But I've just told you *I'm* one,' he jeered softly.

'You just told me you'd picked out your wife.'

'But would you have considered me had I been free?'

'No, I wouldn't, so you can stop looking so sardonic.' She gave a sad, scornful laugh. 'I don't want to hurt your feelings, but I was wary of you from the first minute.'

'Do you know why?' As she had come to a definite halt, Thorn continued the search for the rest of the eggs.

'Self-protection. I sensed exactly that you were up to no good.'

'Idiotic girl!'

Susan made no reply. It didn't seem possible she had only met him a couple of days ago. There had to be some kind of black magic about it, because she completely accepted him as someone who was going to profoundly affect her life. To take her beloved Cobalt Downs from her? To woo and win her sister? She wasn't quite certain which way it would come, but it would.

CHAPTER FIVE

JUST as he had breezed in, Thorn Sinclair drove out on the following Wednesday morning. It was a neat bit of reconnaissance, Susan thought. Spy out the land and plan for what lay ahead.

'Shall we be seeing you again, Mr Sinclair?' she asked with some of his own suaveness, and if she caught the answering glint in his eyes, Patricia had to content herself with the smiling: 'Very possibly.'

It wasn't until quite late at night that Patricia decided to peer in Susan's door.

'Are you asleep, Sue?'

Susan, who had been dreaming, started up and looked towards the illumination. 'What's the matter?'

'I said are you asleep?'

'Positively. I *was*, yes.'

'Can't we have a talk?'

'At this hour?' Susan switched on the bedside lamp.

'Well, I can't sleep.'

'You want to try counting fences.'

'I've been going over and over things in my mind,' said Patricia, and for a slender girl sank very heavily into a chair. 'In the night-time things are so much worse.'

'Hey?' This brought forth all Susan's attention. 'There's nothing bothering you, is there?' She was sitting bolt upright now, thinking all kinds of terrible things.

'Yes, there is.' Patricia sighed deeply. 'Obviously I can't speak to Mummy.'

'Oh, get it out, Paddy,' Susan begged. Was Patricia going to tell her something she couldn't bear to hear?

'It's about Thorn.'

'It would have to be,' Susan said grimly.

'Why are you speaking like that?' Patricia glanced at her. 'Isn't he just the most wonderful man you've ever met? A man to dream about?'

'He's very attractive, yes.' Susan took a deep breath.

'Sue,' Patricia looked up and her eyes were very large and soft, 'I think I'm in love.'

'Oh, do be reasonable, Paddy. You can't be!'

'I *am*.' Patricia was very nearly angry. 'Surely I'd know if I'm in love or not?'

'In my view, you're simply fascinated. He's a very sophisticated, clever and highly literate man. I suppose you could be in love with a man like that.'

'Oh, I *am*!'

'Not like poor old Brett Casey, I hope?'

'You're joking!' Patricia said simply. 'Brett was just a boy. Thorn is a man.'

'Much too old for you. Too old and too worldly. Have you ever thought he's probably had affairs with dozens of women? You're a sweet country girl, and heaven knows, he's extremely sexy. Honestly, Paddy, if you get a crush on Thorn Sinclair, you're quite deranged.'

'But he likes me,' Patricia said shortly. 'He paid me compliments all the time.'

'Did he?' Susan said darkly. 'What kind of compliments?'

'Oh, just little things, but all the time,' Patricia murmured ruminatively. 'I know he thinks I'm lovely.'

'You *are* lovely.' Susan vigorously nodded her

tousled head. 'But surely you didn't believe all this twaddle, Paddy?'

'Why should it be twaddle?' Patricia demanded, obviously overwrought. 'I loathe it when you're so ... blunt. I'm twenty-four, and as Mummy says, as beautiful as a painting, why shouldn't a man fall in love with me? Oh, *do* stop looking at me like that!'

'Paddy,' Susan clasped her hands and looked down at them, 'I think he likes you very much. He finds you charming, as well he might, but I don't think you should allow yourself to fall in love with him. Women might be his forte, for all we know. The next time he comes he might bring some glorious, decadent redhead. We know absolutely nothing about him.'

'Mummy likes him,' Patricia said miserably. 'Mummy always knows quality.'

'Paddy dear,' Susan said slowly, 'I love you too much to feed a fantasy. I don't blame you for being attracted to him, but don't for Pete's sake read a lot into a few compliments. He didn't try to kiss you, did he?'

'He didn't get a chance.' Patricia flushed rosily.

'What do you mean? You turned his advances aside?'

'I mean he has too much finesse.'

'I don't understand.' Susan hopped out of bed and began to pace around the room in an agitated manner. 'Did he say – do – anything that made you optimistic?'

'I'm not completely a fool, Susan,' Patricia said sharply. 'I know when a man's attracted to me. Mummy has very sensitive antennae too.'

'A useful thing to have when it's working right. Oh, I don't know, Paddy. He could be interested in you. Who knows?'

'Aren't you a strange girl!' Patricia said primly. 'I mean, if I get married off, you'll have your chance.'

'Now what's that supposed to mean?' Susan came back to bed.

'Well, Sue,' Patricia said a little wryly, 'I've always been the pretty one. The one with the sweet nature.'

'Gosh, I'm finding this conversation awful! Of course you're pretty. You're lovely—at the same time I can think of plenty of times you haven't been sweet.'

'He's going to come back, isn't he, Sue?' Patricia continued, ignoring her. 'You could see how much he enjoyed his stay.'

'Oh, he'll come back all right,' said Susan, frowning. 'I haven't told you before, but he's at the head of some kind of syndicate that's going to turn the valley into a great big glorious country club. Golf, tennis, squash, a polo complex—you name it.'

'Stop!' Patricia spread her hands wide. 'You mean to say you knew all this and you didn't tell Mummy and me?'

'I'm telling you now, and I guess Mr Sinclair will get around to telling you himself.'

'Good gracious!' Patricia was finding it difficult to remain calm. She stood up, looking very Madonna-like in her blue silk robe. 'Don't you see that you should have told us?'

'Actually I think Mr Sinclair wanted to keep it secret,' Susan explained.

'Then why on earth would he tell you?'

'Well, it is odd, Paddy, but people do confide in me. It must be my face—friendly.'

'You can't keep things hidden like that from Mummy,' Patricia reproached her. 'Of course we

LOVE BEYOND REASON

There was a surprise in store for Amy!

Amy had thought nothing could be as perfect as the days she had shared with Vic Hoyt in New York City—before he took off for his Peace Corps assignment in Kenya.

Impulsively, Amy decided to follow. She was shocked to find Vic established in his new life...and interested in a new girl friend.

Amy faced a choice: be smart and go home...or stay and fight for the only man she would ever love.

MAN OF POWER

Sara took her role seriously

Although Sara had already planned her escape from the subservient position in which her father's death had placed her, Morgan Haldane's timely appearance had definitely made it easier

All Morgan had asked in return was that she pose as his fiancée. He'd confessed to needing protection from his partner's wife, Louise, and that part of Sara's job proved easy

But unfortunately for Sara's heart, Morgan hadn't told her about Monique...

THE LEO MAN

"He's every bit as sexy as his father!"

Her grandmother thought that description would appeal to Rowan, but Rowan was determined to avoid any friendship with the arrogant James Fraser.

Aboard his luxury yacht, that wasn't easy. When they were all shipwrecked on a tropical island, it proved impossible.

And besides, if it weren't for James, none of them would be alive. Rowan was confused. Was it merely gratitude that she now felt for this strong and rugged man?

THE WINDS OF WINTER

She'd had so much— now she had nothing

Anne didn't dwell on it, but the pain was still with her—the double-edged pain of grief and rejection.

It had greatly altered her; Anne barely resembled the girl who four years earlier had left her husband, David. He probably wouldn't even recognize her—especially with another name.

Anne made up her mind. She just *had* to go to his house to discover if what she suspected was true...

Your Romantic Adventure Starts Here.

These FOUR free Harlequin Romance novels allow you to enter the world of romance, love and desire. As a member of the Harlequin Home Subscription Plan, you can continue to experience all the moods of love. You'll be inspired by moments so real...so moving...you won't want them to end. So start your own Harlequin Romance adventure by returning the reply card below. <u>DO IT TODAY!</u>

TAKE THESE 4 BOOKS AND TOTE BAG FREE!

Mail to: Harlequin Reader Service
2504 W. Southern Avenue, Tempe, AZ 85282

YES, please send me FREE and without obligation my 4 Harlequin Romances. If you do not hear from me after I have examined by 4 FREE books, please send me the 6 new Harlequin Romances each month as soon as they come off the presses. I understand that I will be billed only $9.00 for all 6 books. There are no shipping and handling nor any other hidden charges. There is no minimum number of books that I have to purchase. In fact, I can cancel this arrangement at any time. The first 4 books and the tote bag are mine to keep as FREE gifts, even if I do not buy any additional books.

116-CIR-EANY

NAME   (please print)

ADDRESS   APT. NO.

CITY   STATE   ZIP

Signature (If under 18, parent or guardian must sign).

PRINTED IN U.S.A

BUSINESS REPLY CARD

First Class   Permit No. 70   Tempe, AZ

POSTAGE WILL BE PAID BY ADDRESSEE

Harlequin Reader Service
2504 W. Southern Avenue,
Tempe, Arizona 85282

NO POSTAGE
NECESSARY
IF MAILED
IN THE
UNITED STATES

knew he had money, but I never really thought he was a millionaire.'

'We don't really know that he is.'

'Of course he is,' Patricia said scornfully. 'I think I'll wake Mummy up. She'll be in a frenzy.'

'Why don't you inflict it on her in the morning?' Susan yawned.

'She always told me I should marry a millionaire!' Susan announced, her lovely face blazing.

'And now one has actually dropped in. You should never lose each other. Come to think of it, you could work out a deal like in the old days. In return for your hand, he can restore Cobalt Downs to what it was.'

'Don't be mad, Sue,' Patricia said abstractedly, looking ahead to the future. 'When I'm married, I won't be living here. I want to move out into the world. I want to *be* someone. Mrs Thorn Sinclair!' she added in a voice of total self-absorption.

'Gosh, it really is true, isn't it?' said Susan. 'A lady's imagination is very rapid; it jumps from admiration to love, from love to matrimony in a moment. Mr Darcy, you'll find—Jane Austen.'

'Haven't you forgotten about love at first sight?' Patricia challenged, fired up with emotion.

'Describe it.'

'I just have.'

'You're Shakespeare-mad. Remember he said as well, violent delights have violent ends.'

'Rubbish!'

'I think it's probably true. He was a pretty smart old boy and he seems to have said it all.' Susan knelt up on the bed and began to declaim in her best voice. 'It is *too* rash, *too* unadvised, *too* sudden, too like the lightning, which doth cease . . .'

'If you've *quite* finished!' Patricia lurched forward and pushed her. 'How can I expect you to understand? You've never been in love in your life.'

'No,' Susan bounced back again, 'but I have a fair idea of violent delight.'

'I don't believe you. You simply don't *know* anybody like that.'

'I know Thorn Sinclair. My eyes are every bit as good as yours—better. I can see the mind behind the manner ticking over. If he's smitten with anything, it's the property.'

'And *me*!' Patricia persisted, very vehemently for her. 'I have a great deal to offer.'

'A golden girl.' Susan lay back on the pillow. 'All I can tell you, Paddy, is that it's early days yet. You've only just met him, and I can't help thinking his interest in all of us, you particularly, if you like, is motivated by self-interest.'

'You've always tried to damage my pride,' Patricia said tearfully. 'Look at the dreadful way you went on about Brett Casey. You told me he'd made a pass at you simply out of spite.'

'Do you mind if I go to bed, Paddy?' Susan wailed. '*I'm* the one who milks the cows in the morning, not you.'

'Well, someone's got to do it.' Patricia turned towards the door. 'I need new clothes, Susan. I look so awful!'

'All right. I'm going into the city to sell a painting on Wednesday—that's if I don't drop dead in the meantime from overwork. You can have some money then, but we won't be able to replace the John Glover.'

'Hang John Glover!' shrugged Patricia. Just like that.

On the Wednesday, Susan made the almost two-hour journey into the city in her grandfather's old Daimler. It still ran very sweetly and Spider had polished it to a high shine. It was a glorious day, blue and golden, and now the bauhinia trees lined the route, their bare branches smothered in orchid-like blossom. They were spectacular in flower, but of all the colours she thought she loved the white the most—impossibly ethereal. Like Patricia in a wedding dress. Poor Paddy! She really wasn't meant to hide her light beneath a bushel. She was unquestionably meant for better things. One had to be fair about it. The Glover should bring over the twenty thousand dollar mark and Patricia had already pointed out that people were more important than possessions and sentimentality could go hang.

The dealer, guessing she had to sell, began to haggle.

'It's not exactly the best time to sell, Miss Drummond. Things are rather quiet. My best clients are rather preoccupied with their tax and one thing and another.'

'Surely a big company could buy it for their boardroom? Write it off as some kind of tax deduction?'

'Well, as to that or not——' The dealer smiled inanely, telling just by looking at Susan that she really did need the money. Once the Miss Drummonds had been exquisitely dressed, but apart from her looks, which he had always fancied, Miss Susan Drummond was very unremarkably turned out. In fact, he could see a ladder in her stocking, but all the same, beautiful legs. 'Perhaps I could get fifteen or sixteen thousand dollars out of one of them.'

'For me, you mean, or do you still take your commission?'

'Well let's say eighteen and a half, and I take my commission out of that.'

'I'm terribly sorry. It's just no deal.' Susan cut short the bargaining and began to shake out the brown wrapping paper. 'This is a good Glover. You could hang it on your wall for twenty-five thousand and get it. I'm prepared to take twenty thousand. I know it's below your usual commission, but my family have been dealing with yours for a very long time.'

'Wouldn't I be the first to admit it!' The dealer rolled his eyes, then brought them back to eye Susan rather warily. 'I take it you'll be coming to me should you ever wish to dispose of your major paintings?'

'Certainly. If we can do business together.' She nodded her head. 'Obviously one never wants to sell, but there's always some kind of a demand on money.'

'Yes, indeed.' The dealer moved around his desk and offered her coffee. 'My father used to tell me your grandfather used to trot you around the galleries from when you were two years old?'

'Actually it was a little later than that. He put me on a pony when I was two.'

'Gracious!' That seemed to cut short the conversation.

Twenty minutes later Susan emerged from that very luxurious office and found her way down the long flight of staris. Not to worry, she thought. She had really loved that Glover. It had hung above a certain console for as long as she could remember, and she had a cheque for twenty thousand dollars in her handbag—a drop in the ocean if it was ever going to save Cobalt Downs, but at least Mamma and Paddy would be happier, and Peter had to get his share. She was meeting him for lunch.

With time to spare she had her hair trimmed, shampooed and blow-dried, and the difference it made left her all the more conscious that she had been looking rather dreary of late. Her rust printed cotton was fresh and pretty, but by no means a stylish, individual look. In fact the hairdresser had pressed her encouragingly by the shoulders and told her: 'You could look a knock-out with the right clothes!'

It wasn't easy to think of oneself, when there were so many other things to think about. Geoff had been right when he said the homestead was starting to get that vaguely 'neglected' look. The trouble was it cost so very much to maintain. By ordinary suburban standards, it was almost Inveraray Castle, and all things considered, quite beyond their present resources. Perhaps Thorn Sinclair could be persuaded to marry one of them. Susan laughed aloud at the very idea.

Spring sales were everywhere! Mamma and Paddy would have had the most wonderful day, only they didn't really like sales. Exclusive boutique shopping was the key to their personalities, but some of the big department stores offered designer clothes.

Eventually, because she was half-consciously really looking, she found a really smart dress that would make Peter proud of her. It was white, heavy cotton, the bodice hand-painted in an abstract design, the pale pink, gold and orange picked up in a long, wide sash that wrapped twice around her narrow waist which the salesgirl tied into a silk fringed bow.

'Golly, haven't you a tiny waist!' she exclaimed.

'Lots of exercise.' Susan smiled at her, thoroughly relaxed. 'It's a swish kind of dress, isn't it?'

'Especially when you can knot the sash like that.' The salesgirl, pretty but rather plump, stood back admiring. 'A genuine bargain too, you know. Of course you're only size six. You get lots of bargains in the small sizes. It would look terrific with toning shoes.'

'Then I'd better buy them, because I'm going to keep the dress on. I'm having lunch.'

'Your boy-friend?'

'My brother.'

'I bet you've got lots of boy-friends?' The salesgirl deftly snipped off tickets. 'I lead a terribly dreary life in a dingy old flat. I don't know what I'd do without my Harlequins.'

'Heavens, Susy, don't you look smart!' Peter stood back regarding her with his dazzling blue eyes.

'I've been having fun shopping.' In full view of the mall she hugged him to her and kissed him. 'How I've missed you, my clever brother!'

'I've missed you too,' he seconded with deep affection. 'Funny how we've always been so close. Paddy's great, but she's never been the pal you are. Tell me, are they well? How's Mamma?'

'Longing for the weekend you'll come home.'

'I'll try to make it soon.' Peter sounded guarded. 'You know, Susy, you look absolutely beautiful. What have you been doing to your hair?'

'Been to the hairdressers,' Susan boasted. 'Bought a new dress.'

Impulsively Peter caught her hand. 'Let's have lunch somewhere special. You look too good for McDonalds.'

'Surely we weren't going there?'

'That's where *I* go when I want a meal.'

'Mamma would be shocked. Eat up your veggies. You know you need fresh fruit and vegetables if you're going to avoid trouble.'

'Sure, but it's too much trouble cooking.'

'And you're going to be a doctor. Mamma's right,' Susan said firmly, suddenly seeing him on a steady diet of hamburgers. 'If we'd only put into practice what we know!'

'Let's put it into practice now.' Peter, tall and young-man lean and genuinely unconscious of his dazzling good looks, hooked his arm through his sister's and turned her about. 'What do you say to Luciano's?'

'Si!' The expression on her face was radiant. 'I love Italian food.'

'And they're the best restauranteurs in town.'

'What about money?' Susan began to check herself.

'I've got enough. I work as a drinks waiter six nights a week. Don't tell Mamma, but I kinda need the extra money.'

Susan waited until they were seated in the very delightful courtyard setting before she told him her news.

'You'll be pleased to hear I have some money for you.' She opened her handbag, took out the cheque and passed it to him.

'What's this?' Peter frowned.

'I had to sell a picture.'

'Which one?' Peter asked gently, staring past her.

'A Glover. You know, the one over the console.'

'But I can manage, Susy!' He leaned over and caught her hand.

'Paddy wants some new clothes,' she explained, 'and Mamma is getting very restive.'

'Paddy wants some new clothes—yuk! Doesn't Paddy think of anything but throwing things on?'

'She's a beautiful girl, Peter. She's entitled to a good time. It hasn't been that lately, and I think they blame me for it. I'm the one who's trying to hold on to the property when a lot of the time I know it's a losing battle. If I started stripping the house of all its beautiful things it could never be quite the same. In any case, I don't think of them as mine or ours, but rather your children, my children, Paddy's children. The next generation and the one after that.'

'Sometimes I think Grandpa settled you for life,' Peter said reflectively. 'You're the only one of us with that sense of heritage. I love Cobalt Downs, who wouldn't, but it's not the big thing in my life. I want to go doctoring. I want to help people—cure them. I want to be a surgeon. Paddy wants to be a society hostess in the grand tradition—something Mamma never had enough time to play out. They both want to go back to the grand old pastoral days when rich squatters sat on their splendid properties and ruled their own kingdoms. Mamma really expected the Cobalt Downs of Grandpa's day, but we won't see the like of that again. Dad paid the price for trying to keep it on. I can't bear to think of you working so hard.'

'It's my decision, Peter,' Susan said gently.

'I wish I could do something to help you, but it will be years yet,' he sighed.

'Just you turn into a fine doctor—that's enough.'

'Damn it, it isn't!' Peter suddenly looked unhappy.

'Now stop that!' Susan, as usual, had to take charge. 'We've been over all this before. I could make it a lot easier for you right now by selling out. I even know someone who wants to buy. Someone with *real* money.'

'Oh?' Peter looked up, diverted. 'Who?'

'Ever heard of a man called Thorn Sinclair?'

'No.' Peter shook his blond head.

'He's behind the syndicate that bought the McKenzie property.'

'I hate developers,' said Peter, and made way for the waiter to set down his entrée.

'Looks good.' Susan looked up to smile.

'The next course will be even better.' The waiter had beautiful, melting black eyes.

'Anyway, what are they going to turn it into?' Peter forked into his pasta with his favourite *pescatore* sauce.

'Apparently the golfing holiday of a lifetime.' Susan looked from Peter's steaming plate to hers, *fegatini di pollo*.

'*Golfing?*' Peter even put his fork down.

'That's right.'

'But that's marvellous!'

'Really?' Susan's voice was lame, but her green eyes glittered. 'I think it's dreadful, people tramping all over the valley.'

'What a frightful little countrywoman you are, to be sure!'

'Am I?' Susan felt a quiver of hurt.

'Time can't stand still, Susy. Even for you. Golf is a great game. Why, I'd even play there myself. Can you imagine how beautiful it would be? We have National Parks all around us, the lakes and the ranges. If they manage to design it to blend perfectly with the environment it would be simply superb.'

If she had expected fellow feeling, Susan was disappointed. 'You mean you think it's a good idea?'

'Better,' Peter pushed enthusiastically through the spaghetti, rolling it like a long-time expert. 'It's *great*! In fact, now that I come to think of it, probably a terrific natural land site. I mean, look what they'll have to create from—wide fairways, high, wooded hills, a few ravines, lakes, well bunkered, elevated greens.'

'I get the picture,' sighed Susan.

'Eat up!' her brother urged.

'Actually I might find it more acceptable if I played golf,' she mused.

'You should take it up,' Peter nodded his head sagely. 'You're a natural athlete, and you can use Grandpa's clubs.'

'Except I'm five feet two and he was a foot taller. Surely wrong clubs? Even *I* know that.'

'You can practise with them, surely?'

'I'll think about it when I have the time.'

'You're a great girl, Susy.' Peter signalled to the hovering waiter they were ready for more wine. 'Why haven't I heard of this before?'

'I only heard myself. And that's not all.' Susan declined a second glass. Peter had lectures, but she had to keep going. 'Thorn Sinclair is actually Sir Ian Thornton's grandson?'

'Good grief, not the man who won the Melbourne Cup?'

'Because he had the great good fortune to be running a Cobalt Downs breed horse.'

'I've heard it's a small world,' said Peter. 'Fancy that!'

'Of course, what he would really like to do is buy *us* out,' Susan added.

'What absolute cheek!'

'Yes, it *is*.' Susan was delighted they had struck a common chord.

'Of course, we could ask a fortune!' Peter began to see the business side of it almost against his will. 'Think of it, Susy—instead of trying to hold on to the crumbling old manor, we'd be rich!'

'Personally I would vote for the manor and be poor.'

'Look, *eat* that,' Peter told her. 'Nothing's cheap, and you look as if you could do with a good feed.'

Delicious though it was, Susan had to fork into it gamely. 'He was telling me he would want to run it as Grandpa used to, breeding horses for the racetracks. Great horses, and Cobalt Downs is magnificent country for them.'

'Oh, Susy,' Peter looked across at her, with blue, compassionate eyes, 'wouldn't you love that? It's just perfectly your world.'

'And it's going to *stay* mine!'

'All right, pet,' Peter said quickly.

'Would you sell?' she demanded.

'Darling girl, I'd *have* to,' he said gently.

'But you'd never vote against me?'

'No.' Peter shook his head. 'Not me, Susy. In some ways, you're like a rare plant. Take you away from your natural environment and I think you'd sicken and die.'

'So it's two against two.'

'I suppose he's well up in years with a large family, this Sinclair?'

'On the contrary, he's a thirty-four-year-old bachelor with the looks of a staggeringly handsome buccaneer.'

'My word, even I feel a thrill!' Peter drew back as the waiter deftly collected their plates. 'Has Paddy given him one of her terribly ladylike come-ons?'

'She thinks he's in love with her,' Susan said, rather sadly.

'Oh, hell!' Peter looked at her in blank astonishment, then laughed. 'It's not surprising

really. Paddy thinks everyone is in love with her.
But it doesn't happen that way. They fall in love
with you.'

'I'm fine as I am,' Susan said shortly, 'a
vinegary spinster.'

'Not you, sweetie, you're not the type. Really I
suppose Paddy is better-looking than you are, but
personality has rather more to do with attraction
than long golden hair and big blue eyes. Why
doesn't Paddy settle for good old Geoff?' he went
on. They're really very well suited. He'll continue
to think her perfect until the day he dies, and
Paddy thrives on love and admiration.'

'Presently she's in love with Mr Sinclair,' Susan
told him.

'Frankly, if he's a buccaneer,' Peter gave her a
sharp glance, 'he'll be looking at you. You're the
sexy one.'

'And I haven't the stamina for passionate love
affairs. My love affair is with Cobalt Downs.'

'Ah, here he comes with the main course!' Peter
breathed with satisfaction. 'This has to be one of
the best Italian restaurants in Australia!'

Susan didn't have the heart to bother him
further. The waiter set down their *pollo alla
cacciatora* and *vitello tonnato*, and Peter looked at
both dishes with obvious pleasure. Not surprising
really, considering his steady diet of Big-Macs.

Susan declined a third course, but Peter had
already decided on a ravishing slice of Mamma's
Cake. It was an incredibly luscious dessert cake,
and Susan was at last persuaded by the very
charming waiter to at least try an exotic biscuit
with her coffee.

'Gosh, I'll remember this meal forever!' Peter
exclaimed afterwards. 'Listen, sweetie, I'll have to
rush.' He pulled out a wallet and ruffled through

the notes. 'All things considered, this is the best way I know of spending money.'

'Young man,' she laughed. 'Unfillable! Oh, it's lovely to see you, Peter. I love you so much.'

'And I love you too, Susy.' Peter wouldn't allow his eyes to sting, but he swallowed. 'I've been meaning to tell you something, but I kept it for the last minute. I've met a girl. . . .'

'You *can't* meet a girl, Peter!' Susan thought of the sacrifices to keep him at university.

'It's all right!' Peter held up his hand. 'You'll like her, Susy, and she'll like you. You're much the same—gay and vital, lovely impulses, sweet.'

'Oh, Peter,' Susan bent her head, 'you sound as if you're in love with her.'

'I am.'

'Oh, Peter!' Susan said again. How could she be wholehearted about keeping Cobalt Downs when her family needed money?

'She's in my year too. In fact, she's expected to top our final year. She's brilliant. She's going to specialise in pediatrics.'

'What's her name?'

'Elizabeth Mallory. Isn't that beautiful?'

'It is rather nice,' Susan smiled.

'I wanted to bring her home maybe the weekend after next, but you know what Mamma's like! She can't let anyone else do the talking.'

'If you're really serious about Elizabeth, Peter,' Susan said a little sternly, 'she'll have to get used to Mamma. She means well. She adores you.'

'But really, Susy, you know very well she does go on. Then Paddy can be a bit ridiculous from time to time—all that to the manor born stuff. Elizabeth is absolutely lovely and so clever, but her people are just ordinary. Nice people, I like them, but they live in an ordinary house and they have ordinary jobs.'

'Hell, Peter, don't tell me!' she protested. 'I'm not a snob.'

'But Mamma is, and so is Paddy. I can't have Elizabeth being patronised.'

'Peter darling,' Susan took his hand, 'if she's all the things you say she is, I expect she'll handle Mamma and Paddy beautifully. There's no point in worrying. Mamma is never cruel.'

'She can be,' said Peter, looking solemn. 'Remember the way she baited that poor Mrs Mullins?'

'At any rate, not until after dinner. Don't worry, Peter, if you want to bring your lovely Elizabeth, just let me know. I'll do everything I can to make the visit a success—and besides, we have a little money. I'll bank this cheque and send you your share.'

'Keep it,' Peter told her firmly. 'I told you, I get by.'

'No, I'll send it,' said Susan. 'Or keep it until you come. Only don't for heaven's sake think of getting married yet, Peter. You're so young and you're not even through, and. . . .'

'I didn't say I'm getting married yet, Susy,' all at once Peter looked very mature, 'but I've definitely settled on the girl and she on me. When you fall in love, you'll *know*. I shouldn't mention this, I'm so modest, but I have mysterious power over women. They fall in the hallways every time I pass by. Elizabeth says she's never seen a guy so indifferent to his own looks.'

'Ah well, you grew up in a good-looking household. Paddy is a genuine beauty, I'm not too bad and Mamma is a very superior-looking woman.'

'Handy, for putting people down.'

They parted on the pavement with more hugs

and kisses, and as Susan turned away, still smiling with tenderness she saw Thorn Sinclair step out of a chauffeur-driven Rolls.

It was a full moment before she could move, and when the paralysis died out of her limbs his look of imposing, businesslike formidability gave way to recognition.

'Miss Drummond!' He eyed her with the now familiar amusement and mockery. 'How you do stand out in a crowd!'

'You too.' She gave him her hand but smiled sharply. 'I suppose you do this sort of thing often, step out of a chauffeured Rolls?'

'Only when I'm in town. I rarely take it out into the hills. Don't trust it on all those potholed dirt roads.'

'I expect you'll fix all that when you tear up the valley,' she observed.

'Doesn't take much to start you off, does it?' His silver eyes flashed in a way she remembered.

'Some people never learn.' Today he looked impossibly handsome, arrogant and elitist in his fine city clothes, things she thought she deplored, but sensuality was firing her blood.

He stood at his impressive height looking down at her. 'You've cut your hair.'

'Mm. Like it?'

'I had a polo pony once with just that black, gleaming coat.'

'Thanks!'

'Don't let it annoy you. I loved that pony.' Passers-by were staring at them curiously and he took her arm and moved her along ahead. 'What brings you to town? I didn't think anything could ever get you away from Cobalt Downs.'

She moved smoothly beside him. 'A little business, then lunch with Peter.'

'Peter?' The frown was unmistakable. 'Oh, Peter, your brother.'

'What would you have said had it been Peter, my lover?'

Boldly the silver eyes travelled over her. 'No lovers yet.'

'Then why did you frown?'

He gave a hard, abrupt laugh. 'I couldn't place the name for a moment, but obviously you've enjoyed yourself.'

'Yes. I don't see half enough of him.' Suddenly, because she had just become aware of it, she burst out: 'Where are you taking me?'

'To my office. I thought you might like to see our plans for the valley.'

'*Here?*' she managed finally, looking up at the tall building.

'Yes, here.'

'Thornton Towers?' She clutched his arm.

'Thornton Towers. Come along, Susan. You can't stand out on the pavement with your mouth open.'

They rode up in the lift to the top floor where the executive offices unfolded. 'Magnificent!' she exclaimed.

'I knew you'd like it.'

'Oh, good afternoon, Mr Sinclair!' An elegant, middle-aged secretary got off her chair. 'Shall I tell Mr Grantly you're back?'

'I'll ring when I want to see him, Mrs Randall,' Thorn Sinclair cut her off pleasantly. 'Coffee for two, if you please. I don't want to be disturbed for an hour.'

'Yes, sir.'

'I'd hate to work in an office,' Susan murmured as that elegant lady rushed to obey his every whim. 'There's no way you could make me act the tea-lady.'

'No, we could only give you notice. Come this way, Miss Drummond.'

Inside the splendid, big office Susan released her breath. 'You mean you *are* Thornton Enterprises?'

'Anything else you would like to know?'

'No wonder you could afford to buy the McKenzie place!'

'Chickenfeed, my dear Miss Drummond. Please sit down, and then I can admire your beautiful legs. It's not often I get to see them.'

Slowly, solemnly, she advanced to a side table set with an elaborate and complex plan. 'Is this the valley resort?'

His eyes, as brilliantly clear as diamonds, met hers. 'I promise you it's been expertly designed to blend in perfectly with its beautiful natural environment.'

'Poor Miss McKenzie! I guess if they'd buried her in the valley somebody would be hitting off her tombstone?'

'Trust you to think of that!'

Susan's mind was in chaos. She had always thought herself the steady, responsible, reliable one, the one who could focus on what men were really after, when it just so happened she was as dithery about Thorn Sinclair as ever Paddy was. Just standing small and quiet beside him was a tremendous drain on her emotional reserves. The steady was getting mislaid somewhere. She even wished he would hold her, kiss her to a bitter-sweet numbness. She was terrified of raising her eyes unless the expression in them would be naked.

'Well, what do you think?' he asked. 'You aren't, I believe, struck dumb?'

'It looks terribly, terribly professional and a much bigger project than you led me to believe.'

'Many millions, Miss Drummond. There's not

going to be any other resort in Australia like it.'

'And you plan to live on the other side of the valley?'

'Now let's not be hasty! I only said you had beautiful legs.'

She totally ignored the mockery. 'What are all these buildings?'

'Country Club, Lodge, private self-contained villas. That's for our resident pro and his family. We'll have international stars coaching from time to time. This here, as you can see, is the Tennis Village. Twelve all-weather courts, championship centre court. Restaurants, pools, alfresco bars, over here, polo fields . . .'

'Trail rides?'

'Yes. Not everyone will want to play golf or tennis. Non-players will have plenty to do. It's going to offer the whole package without making it that hard tourist stuff. We'll be spending a tremendous amount of money just keeping it all natural. The top town-planners, landscape designers, architects, engineers, you name them—we have the best in the country.'

'And it's going to happen right now?'

'It's going to *start* happening very soon. You realise, of course, it will probably take two years or more, but it has to be developed in the right way.'

'Thank God!' Susan exclaimed.

'You had to say it, didn't you?'

'Yes.' Susan bit her lip. 'I used to ride all over the McKenzie place. Miss McKenzie always used to ask me in for a huge afternoon tea. The poor old darling scarcely ate a bite, but she used to get her housekeeper to make an absolute feast for me. I don't believe she would have liked this at all.'

'I realise you can't be tactful all the time,' said Thorn drily. 'Miss McKenzie, great lady, was ninety-four when she died. Her kind of world has gone just as yours is getting away from you. The cost of holding on to your private kingdom comes very high. Who can afford it, Susan? Only millionaires.'

'You know how I feel about millionaires.'

'*Look* at me when you say that!'

'All right!' She swung up her glossy head and tilted her chin. 'Don't delude yourself into thinking you're going to talk me into selling.'

'Not with your fighting spirit. It's amazing how tenacious the old clans are.' He put his two hands on her shoulders and despite herself she gasped.

'Your secretary will be coming with the coffee!'

'She's not my secretary. My secretary is young and beautiful.'

'Now why didn't I realise that!'

'Okay, so why are you trembling? You seem to do it every time I touch you, brush your hand.'

'If I told you, you'd be twice as conceited.'

'I'm not conceited at all,' he drawled.

'And your timing is terrible!' she said airily when a knock came at the door.

'Keep up the chatter, Susan,' he released her unhurriedly and leaned back against the desk, 'I could shock the hell out of you, and you damn well know it.'

'I'm sorry, Mr Sinclair. . . .' An elegant, upswept head appeared around the door.

'No, please come in, Mrs Randall. I'm dying for that cup of coffee.'

'Fine, sir.'

Susan had never heard that tone of deference, not since the days of Grandpa, who although extremely egalitarian, never permitted sloppy disrespect.

'Lovely, thank you.' Susan looked at the woman and smiled.

'Just one telephone call I've got to make,' Thorn Sinclair told her after Mrs Randall had gone.

'Shall I step outside the door or just put my hands over my ears?'

'For my sake—stay here.' He sat down and dialled the number, then when the number connected, turned sideways in the swivel chair. 'Hi, Vicky,' he said, half smiling.

And that's that! Susan thought. No one spoke to a woman in that special voice unless he made love to her once in a while.

'Uh-huh. . . .'

The sensual quality was disgusting. Susan had the impulse to sip noisily at her coffee, instead she took it in hand and wandered back to the resort plan.

'Oh, he did, did he? Listen, darling. . . .'

Paddy's world would be crashing around her nose if she could hear this drivel. Did he really have to make an intimate phone call with someone else in earshot, or was there method in his madness? Method probably. Mr Thorn Sinclair would have a reason for every move he made. Had he a vague idea that Paddy was seriously attracted to him? Was he conceited enough to think *she* was attracted to him as well? One telephone call to make the message clear?

'Yes, I'll see you tonight. Eight-thirty? Fine. So long, darling.'

Behind her, Susan heard him drop the receiver so casually she turned, very careful to keep her face buttoned-up.

'Is that right for you?' he asked.

'Lovely. Black and strong, the way I like it.'

'Make yourself at home, Susan. You look nervous.'

'I'm sure I don't.' She imitated her mother and walked rather disdainfully to a black leather armchair.

'I almost wish you were a man,' he said.

'Really?' She glanced up, vaguely astonished. 'Why?'

'Little girls tie me in knots.' The hint of mockery was still there but definitely overlaid with seriousness. 'A man in your position I could bargain with, talk over the situation realistically, but with you, emotions run deep.'

'I would have thought exactly the same would apply to a man.'

'Tell me,' he said shrewdly, 'does Peter want to sell the property?'

'Never!' Colour stained her high cheekbones.

'He loves you too much.'

'Yes, he loves me.'

'Patricia told me all about your devotion. Apparently you're his favourite sister?'

'I think he loves us all the same. Certainly he's Mamma's pride and joy.'

'Not Patricia?' He came around to her and settled back against the desk.

'I don't mind if my mother has a special feeling for Paddy,' Susan said. 'This has to be understood. She's the image of Mamma, really, and then again, she's so beautiful. It's difficult not to love a sweet and beautiful human being.'

'Let's see,' he said casually, 'how would we describe you?'

'The only one who wants to hold on to Cobalt Downs,' she said quietly. 'I know my sister told you how she and Mamma feel. Peter, too, has no

fervent desire to hold on at all costs. That burden
has been given to me.'

'*Burden?*' He picked her up very quickly.

'Yes, as well as love of possession. With staff
and a healthy loan there's no reason why I
couldn't make a go of this thing I'm doing, but
even if I did, it wouldn't make Mamma happy.
She loathes people on the property.'

'I'd rather gathered that,' he said drily. 'Your
will, Susan, is bigger than you are. Had you been a
man, had your family been behind you, you might
be able to survive, at least for a while, but
inevitably someone will step in.'

'I suppose so,' she sighed.

'You've gone white,' he observed.

'Do you find it a sheer pleasure to torture?'

'*Susan!*' She discovered she was on her feet. 'I'm
not letting you rush out of here,' Thorn said
harshly.

'I hardly think you can tell me what to do!' It
was the greatest effort to control her voice.

'Don't be silly, Susan.' As before he grasped her
shoulders and very nearly shook her. 'I *don't* want
to hurt you.'

'You *do*.' What were all these terrible shivers
that were running through her? Anger, desire?

'Maybe I *do*.' Heavy lids came down over his
eyes. 'Maybe I'm angry for the same reason you
are. Maybe I'm attracted to you and I don't want
to be. You're hardly more than an infant!'

'Certainly not like the woman you were talking
to.' There, she had said it, like a fool!

'Jealous?' he asked sharply. 'Green eyes?'

She saw it happening, his intention, and though
she arched her head away he caught it and she
closed her eyes.

'Open your mouth to me.'

She took a violent triumph out of keeping her small white teeth clamped shut.

'Susan.' He didn't merely speak her name, but drew her so close against his body, the strong will she boasted of was broken.

'I hate you!' she whispered.

'I don't care.' At first he teased her mouth with his own, fanning sensations along the nerves, then his face drawn in a kind of cruelty he moved his hands over her body and took deep possession of her mouth.

She couldn't twist her head or her body any way. She was pressed to him, almost held off the ground. He was so strong he could do it without effort—crush her. She thought she moaned and he allowed her a little breath, then continued to take all the pleasure he wanted. And pleasure it had to be because she could feel the faint trembling in that lean, hard body.

She didn't know what she wanted him to do to her. But whatever he was doing, it wasn't enough. It was agony, an intense clamouring for rapture that was being denied.

When Thorn finally released her she was gasping, her small head thrown back against his arm. She thought if anyone came to the door, there was nothing she could do. She was shocked at how weak she felt, her body clinging to his as though it was his forever.

'It's all right, don't be frightened. No one will come in.'

A little moan did escape her, muffled in her throat. 'I didn't ask for that, did I?'

'It wasn't necessary to ask, Susan.' His silver eyes were blazing, but his voice was sombre. 'I knew I was going to make love to you at first glance.'

'At first glance you thought I was a boy.'

'Maybe I did until I saw your mouth and your eyes. You disturb me, little Miss Drummond, and I don't like that—not at all.'

'Then why don't you let me go?'

'I'm going to wait until we both stop shaking. Passion is contagious, you know.'

'And just how many women do you feel passionate about?' she asked contemptuously.

'I'm sorry if it makes you uncomfortable, but right at the moment, just you.'

'Don't think I don't know what this is all about!' Susan brought up her elbows and tried to lever them against his locked arms, hopeless, a mixture of torture and ecstasy.

'Why particularly would I want to be attracted to a mere schoolgirl who's determined on ruining all my plans?'

'I'd love to! If it kills me I'm going to hold on to Cobalt Downs.'

'Don't *say* that!' he muttered.

'Yes, I will!'

'And don't you damned well ride Mephisto,' he added. 'Granted you're a fine rider, but he's a rogue. Some days he hates people. Got that? On his vicious day, and how could you expect to know it, he could break your neck.'

'Assuredly what you're trying to do now!'

'It would have helped a great deal, Susan, if your father had put you occasionally across his knee. Like every other week. A value can be placed on Cobalt Downs, but it can never be placed on your life. Can't you see yourself for what you are? Don't you believe it when you see yourself in a photograph? You're just a gallant but rather fragile young girl, not a grazier on the grand plane like your grandfather. He controlled a kingdom, but your father found what it was like trying to keep it, to his cost.'

'Grandpa lost a fortune on his investments!' Susan shouted. 'My father slaved! He worked from morning to night, seven days a week, and it killed him!'

Suddenly she was crying, sobbing bitterly and with an abandon she had never allowed herself in her life. It even seemed to her that once started, she would never be able to stop.

'Cry,' Thorn said. 'Let it work for you.' He was lifting her and as a twist held her cradled in his arms in the armchair she had first taken.

She pressed her knuckles to her mouth and sank her teeth into the bone. If she could just hold on to herself, stop crying. He was destroying her— making her kiss him, making her cry. She rolled her head away, but when she looked up and met his eyes she read in them true compassion.

'Don't ... you ... feel ... sorry ... for ... me.' She spoilt it with a hiccough.

'No.'

'I think it was the wine for lunch.'

'I don't think you've ever cried all your grief out. Forget who I am, Susan—my background, what I'm trying to do. Just lie in my arms for a while and think of me as a friend. I know you need one. More, you need a husband, someone to look after you.'

'I can look after myself!' she said with the appropriate violence.

'You look like a jet-black kitten, with big green eyes.'

She gave a ragged sigh. 'First a polo pony, now a kitten!'

'I'm an animal lover,' Thorn explained.

'Maybe if you could love me, we'll get married.

I'll get to keep Cobalt Downs and you could breed the most magnificent thoroughbreds. I'd help you. I guess the house is big enough for us both to have complete privacy.'

'From each other?'

'Of course.'

'Just to go along with your fantasy what would happen when I wanted to make love to you?'

'It's a business deal I'm suggesting,' she said drily.

'On my *knee*?'

'You're the one who keeps picking me up.'

'Because you're just a kid. Everyone picks little kids up and cuddles them—especially when they're hurt.'

'I'm not hurt. I'm brokenhearted,' Susan told him bitterly.

'I know that.'

'How do *you* know, when no one else does?'

'Oh—the shadows in your eyes. They flit around like goldfish.'

'You're a dangerous man,' she said carefully.

'And you're a very touchy, proud little girl.'

'So how come we're close to each other now?'

'Do you want to move?' Thorn put one hand through her hair.

'I'll have to, even if it takes all the strength I've got.' She struggled a little just as a demonstration, but he merely said languidly:

'There's time.'

'How long?'

'Oh, about ten minutes. After that, I'm going to scoop you up and put you outside the door. I'd really like to kiss you again, but I can see now that would be incredibly foolish. It could get to be a habit.'

'And we don't live in the same world anyway.'

'You mean you won't part with it.'

Susan tilted her head back against his broad shoulder and looked up at him, a near-stranger, yet so familiar, a man in whose arms she knew that paradoxical thing, peace and security, excitement and danger. 'Hey now, Mr Sinclair,' she said gently, 'would *you*?'

CHAPTER SIX

THE fortnight seemed to fly before Peter's visit.
Cobalt Downs had more visitors in the intervening
weekend than it had entertained in the preceding
six months, and if Susan, Annie and Spider were
made joyous by the largely increased takings the
situation was soon explained when one of the
guests referred to the advertisement run for several
days in the leading city newspaper that he, his wife
and family had found so compelling. There had
been a magnificent shot of the house from across
the lagoon and apparently a lot of blurb promising
a real taste of the country for that camping
weekend.

'Sounds like Mr Sinclair!' Spider had laughed,
with open admiration, with Annie smiling indul-
gently and Susan hissing: 'How *dare* he!'

'Dammit, Susy!' Spider had bit out disgustedly.
'Can't you take a little bit o'help?'

'Then why didn't he tell me?'

'You'd probably have said no.'

Maybe she would have. Anyway, it all turned
out to be very enjoyable. As soon as Susan lifted a
finger to do anything, there seemed to be some
nice man or his teenage son right at her shoulder,
offering help, so instead of working hard trying to
ensure that their guests were happy, Susan found
herself very much the one who was entertained.

'This is a card from young Michael,' she said,
coming into the kitchen. 'He wanted to tell us
again that he had a lovely weekend. I suppose
Thorn Sinclair is a maternal cousin. I sort of got

vibrations there. There's this odd little girl running these camping holidays. Get out there and help her.'

'A real gentleman, Mr Sinclair,' said Annie.

'You don't quite understand the situation, Annie. He wants Cobalt Downs no matter how long it takes.'

'Oh yes, maybe he did before he met you. We had a nice long talk.'

'*You* did?' Susan looked at Annie, plump face in astonishment.

'Yes. The kitchen's a great place for a yarn.'

'Good grief!' Susan could see the 'conversation' with a frightful clarity. Annie was convinced she was a little heroine battling against overwhelming odds and pass it on to Thorn Sinclair.

'Your mother's so happy Peter is coming!' Annie looked towards the ceiling and affably rolled her eyes. 'But I don't suppose they'll be two minutes together before the fight's on.'

'I certainly hope not!' Susan took a good pinch of sultanas from Annie's pile of mixed fruit and got a slap on the hand for her trouble. 'Put some cocoa in it, Annie. I love fruit cake when it's rich and dark. I'm praying this weekend is going to be terribly successful. Mamma and Paddy have nice new clothes. You and I have the house looking reasonably spick and span. It will be clear to Elizabeth that we can't get around all of it and the weather is absolutely sparkling. The hills are shining, the air glitters—Cobalt Downs at its best. We'll be full up all along the creek, but it only adds to the festive atmosphere. That young fellow Spider hired for a couple of days has even got the barbecue bins chock full of logs. I hope we paid him enough. He certainly did a lot of work. It must be wonderful to be a man, and so strong.

Spider and I nearly passed out just looking at him go.'

'Well, Spider's no longer the boy he was, even if he stills eats the same. Where do you suppose he puts it?'

'Metabolism, Annie, I'm sorry.' Susan put her arms around Annie's rotund shape and hugged her. 'How do you suppose Mamma is going to react when she sees Peter is really serious about this girl?'

'A girl serious about her precious darling?'

'Perhaps Peter had better jump in first and explain that he and Elizabeth are prepared to wait until they're in a position to marry.'

'As serious as that, is it?' There was concern in Annie's quiet glance.

'I think so,' said Susan. 'His face lit up when he spoke about her. Peter doesn't really change when he settles on something. He's always wanted to be a doctor, and I think he wants Elizabeth in the same way too.'

'Then I sort of feel sorry for her,' said Annie. 'Your mother has always been extremely possessive of Peter—the only son syndrome. I was reading something about it the other day. No girl will be good enough, you know that. Certainly no girl your mother didn't pick herself. She'll want to talk about Elizabeth's family, who they are, what they are—what kind of profession the father is established in. You must know, Susy—the old third degree.'

'I'll be there. I'll divide them up. Peter said she's very clever, and she must be a dedicated girl. It's quite possible she'll be a match for Mamma.'

'Can you remember anyone who has been, then?' Annie asked.

'Strangely enough, only Thorn Sinclair. Mamma was absolutely delighted with him.'

'Then let's all pray and hope she's absolutely delighted with the girl her only son has chosen.'

Peter and Elizabeth drove up Friday evening and as soon as Elizabeth stepped outside the car Susan knew the visit was not going to be a success.

'My goodness, she's untidy!' Patricia exclaimed.

'Does it really matter? Keep your voice down—she'll hear you!' Susan hurried forward down the stairs, while her mother and Patricia stood framed by the splendid porte-cochère.

'Oh, Peter, it's lovely to see you. *Elizabeth*!'

'My sister Susan.' Peter stood beaming while the two girls smiled at each other with spontaneous liking and clasped hands.

'Everything is so beautiful, Susan,' Elizabeth said in a deep, very melodious contralto. She was a tall girl, standing many inches over the petite Susan, her strongly boned, highly intelligent face unpainted, her hair thick and straight and brown, looped into a careless knot, her dress such that it was immediately apparent she had no great interest in clothes, but the overall effect was one of great wholesomeness and character. She wasn't at all what Susan expected. Peter had always been attracted to very pretty girls, but Susan felt extraordinarily relieved. Here was a young woman of character and sympathy and understanding. A woman who would grow with Peter, share a life of dedication and devotion, combine motherhood and a career, make him happy. There was such an intense capability about her, all Susan's sisterly anxieties were removed.

'Welcome to Cobalt Downs!' she said, and the sort of things she had been thinking shone out of her eyes.

Peter looked up swiftly towards the elegant

outlines of his mother and other sister, but they remained poised like Royalty, waiting for the audience to come to them.

'Please come in,' said Susan. 'Don't worry about your suitcase. Peter will bring it up later.'

'Peter has told me so much about you, Susan, I feel I know you already,' Elizabeth smiled.

'He's told me he loves you.' Susan turned and looked directly into Elizabeth's clear grey eyes. She did it deliberately, wanting to bolster Elizabeth's confidence when she was certain now her mother would do everything in her power to break it up.

Elizabeth smiled at her, somehow conveying that she knew what might be ahead of her, and went up the broad flight of stairs unafraid.

'Come to me, darling!' Julia threw out her arms to her son. 'How I've missed you!'

Peter went solemnly into a rather unnerving embrace, a kind of hero's return home, then managed to emerge to perform the introductions.

'How do you do, Miss Mallory,' said Julia in the coldest voice all three of her children had yet heard.

'It's very kind of you to invite me, Mrs Drummond,' Elizabeth said politely.

Sometimes it paid to be tall, Susan thought. Elizabeth certainly carried that off, answering very pleasantly as though she was quite used to mammas from whom lesser girls would have run a mile.

'Actually, my dear,' Julia smiled tightly, 'Peter presented us with a fait accompli, but then we're used to Peter. He's always bringing his ... friends home. Do come in. You may want to rest after your trip. I have so much to catch up on with Peter. There's such an absolute bond between mother and son.'

'Elizabeth never feels tired,' said Peter. 'I want to show her something of the property before it gets dark.'

'But, my dear Peter, you have all weekend for that. You *cannot* want to rush out now. I've had Annie make us some nice tea. Susan can settle Miss Mallory in her room, then she can come down whenever she's ready. There's no use striding down the track. Susan has all those ghastly people blanketed along the creek—I expect you saw all the tents. It makes me want to run away screaming.'

'Actually I think they look quite pretty,' Patricia said unexpectedly. 'Certainly I feel a little better about them than I used to.'

'Come along, Peter,' said Julia, casting her elder daughter a telling look. 'Miss Mallory won't run away, and we must have a little talk. You really must try to write me a letter some time. I'm entitled to know how you're progressing with your studies.

'Oh dear!' Elizabeth said quietly as she walked along the gallery with Susan. 'I don't think your mother was very impressed with me.'

'Maybe she's afraid of you, Elizabeth,' Susan said. 'It could be a fundamental thing. Mothers do look long and hard at the girls their sons choose to love.'

'And he's used to beautiful women, isn't he?' Elizabeth shrugged rather wryly. 'You, your mother, your sister—you're all extremely good-looking. Half the girls I know follow Peter around just hoping he'll look at them, and gosh, he wants *me*. Do you suppose it's my brain that's inspiring him?'

'Brain, body, soul.' Susan opened the door to Elizabeth's bed-sitting room.

'Oh, how lovely!' Elizabeth's face cleared and she walked past Susan into the large, beautifully furnished room. 'I've never been in such a grand house in my life. Peter told me about it often, but the reality far exceeds my mental picture. How on earth do you get around the housework?'

'We don't.'

Elizabeth shot her an amused glance. 'I very much admire what you're doing, you know.'

'I want Drummonds to be here in another hundred years.'

'I can understand that,' said Elizabeth. 'What a beautiful rug!' she added.

'Persian. The Tree of Life,' Susan told her.

'And flowers.' Elizabeth walked to the small circular table where several books were placed and a large silver wine cooler filled with two dozen golden roses. 'How nice!'

'We want you to feel happy here,' Susan smiled.

'You mean *you* want me to, Susan. I could see the surprise in your sister's eyes. A lot of the time, for Peter's sake, I'd like to be lovely to look at, but I guess I'm just a 'brown' girl, if you know what I mean.'

'When you're making Peter so happy and you're so nice to look at and clever? Let's just suppose you were very glamorous. Would Peter love you more?'

'The odd thing is, he thinks I'm lovely,' Elizabeth blushed.

'Why not? You are.'

'If I lost him,' Elizabeth said, 'I could scarcely bear it.' She walked through the open french doors and out on to the verandah, her face a little strained. 'Be my friend, Susan, would you?' She turned and held out a long-fingered hand with obvious supplication, and Susan took it firmly.

'You're worrying about nothing, you know. Mamma can be a little formidable at first, but all she wants is Peter's happiness.'

'And I can make him happy, Susan,' Elizabeth said. 'I *know*. But if your mother really decides she doesn't like me, and she has a strong influence on Peter, I've always known this, it could make it intolerable for me.'

'Of course she's going to like you,' Susan assured her. 'You've got a lot of sense, Elizabeth, I can see that. Just take things quietly. Things will work out, I promise you. You see, Peter has always been . . . one-track, if you like. When he settles on something, that's it. As it turns out, medicine and you.'

'Well, it had better be!' Elizabeth suddenly laughed, a full ringing sound. 'Actually I'm pretty tough, as it happens. I come from a large family.'

'Tell me about them,' Susan invited.

Dinner was worse again, in fact it was horrible in a terribly proper and formal way, and only when Peter jumped up did Julia finally register faint alarm.

'My dear boy, we haven't finished!'

'I am. My nerve is giving out. Come for a walk, Elizabeth. It's terribly stuffy in here.'

Elizabeth excused herself politely and she and Peter moved rather hurriedly through the double cedar doorway and out towards the garden.

'I can't believe Peter could be so rude!' Julia cried, looking from daughter to daughter for affirmation and support.

'Oh, for heaven's sake!' Patricia laughed a little wildly. 'You were the rude one, Mummy. That poor girl! She's very modest and nice, and you heard what Peter said, she's a brilliant student.'

'Are you criticising me?' Julia's blue eyes glittered in outrage.

'I don't want to, Mummy,' Patricia said, her long blonde hair framing her lovely face. 'But really, your manner is freezing! Ask Susan.'

'Susan?' Julia glared across the table.

'There's nothing to be gained creating a situation, Mamma. Peter is really serious this time.'

'Rubbish!' Julia cried piercingly. 'You can't tell me this girl will last. Why, she's plain, and very sloppy in her dress. She couldn't possibly hold him. It's just a passing fancy.'

'Even if it were, and I don't believe it is, don't you think it would be very much better to be pleasant? Even if you have to pretend.'

'I can't. I can't!' Julia put a hand to her aching heart. 'Do you realise they could have plain children? It's like a nightmare! Her mother works behind a counter and her father sells furniture.'

'Does it matter?' Susan asked. 'I believe it's excellent furniture.'

Julia gave a small, pitiful cry. 'Stop! Please stop. In the old days that girl would never have been invited to this house.'

'Oh yes, she would!' said Susan. 'Daddy wasn't a snob, and Grandpa used to have all sorts of people in.'

'Your grandfather was eccentric!' Julia raised her head and pulled at her magnificent sapphire and diamond engagement ring. 'I had such high hopes for my children, but I can see them all coming to nothing. Mr Sinclair seemed to leave in a hurry.'

'He'll be back,' Susan said bluntly.

'Where *is* he?' Julia almost forgot Elizabeth's existence. 'I was absolutely delighted when it seemed he was so attractive to Patricia, but perhaps that was another dream?'

'Oh, come, Mummy! Susan said he'll be back.'

'And how does Susan know so much?' Julia demanded. 'She always was a secretive girl.'

Susan sighed over this and stood up. 'If that was dinner, it was a fiasco. Won't you please be gentle, Mamma, and not hurt Peter and Elizabeth too much? I'm so frightened that if you don't we won't see him at all.'

In fact, Julia did take the warning, and when Peter and Elizabeth finally returned she adopted a much lighter if not joyous tone and in fact went so far as to drop the 'Miss Mallory' for Elizabeth. After all, it was a splendid sort of name.

The next morning Peter and Elizabeth set out early for a long walk together. Elizabeth did not ride, a piece of information Julia had greeted with amazement, indeed she expressed the wish that it might rain.

'He really doesn't care about me at all, does he?' she demanded of her daughters. 'We haven't seen him for weeks, and all he wants to do is be alone with that girl.'

'Yes, but don't you remember what it was like, Mummy?' Patricia asked.

'Indeed I don't. I was brought up to cherish my parents, God rest their souls. I would never have gone off with your father when my clear duty was to remain at home. Peter has told me nothing, absolutely nothing. We've had no conversation at all.'

'What do you think of Elizabeth?' Susan asked Annie as she rinsed the breakfast dishes.

'A very nice girl,' Annie answered after a moment. 'Mind you, she's not what I expected.

Not after the little bits of nothing Peter used to chase after.'

'That was kid stuff,' said Susan. 'He's never really settled on anyone, until Elizabeth. I do wish Mamma could like her more.'

'Well, I don't think your mother would be satisfied with an heiress, but I think she'll come to see gradually that Peter must choose his own wife. She can't do it for him. Do you remember that ghastly mess when she tried to bring Peter and that Stirling girl together?'

'It seems so long ago,' Susan mused. 'Now I'll stack the dishwasher for you, then I must go down and check on our guests—say hello and that sort of thing. We're suddenly becoming very popular.'

'And you know who we have to thank!'

'Miracle worker Sinclair. I wonder what he's up to?'

Susan was on a high hill looking down at the valley when she first spotted the helicopter. She gazed up in a dazed way, shading her eyes with her cupped hands. The distant object grew bigger, correspondingly the whirring sound of the rotor.

'What did I tell you!' she exclaimed aloud. 'Helicopters on the lawn!'

She turned Persian Princess quickly, excitement and anticipation blending with her blood. Speak of the devil and he descended from the sky in a whirring dragon! Of course it was Thorn Sinclair, and he seemed to be delighting in shadowing her galloping progress. It made her go faster, but when she realised the home grounds he was there before her, stepping out of the helicopter and waving.

'Hi there, sonny!'

'I don't think we're ever going to forget that.' She reined in Persian Princess with a featherlight touch. 'Is that your new toy?'

'Handy, isn't it?' He seemed to be examining her as closely as she was examining him. 'I was over the other side of the valley, and I thought I'd just pop in.'

'To see if your ad's working? You could have seen that from the air.'

'Don't say thank you!' he said drily.

'I intend to. Thank you very much, Mr Sinclair. If you let me know the cost of running the advertisement . . .'

'As a matter of fact, I will. Dinner tonight. After all, Patricia has had her turn. How are the family, by the way?'

Her eyes moved over him in her own way, despite herself revelling in the boldness and the breeding, the strength and virility that was so much a part of him. He was wearing an open-necked, short-sleeved blue shirt and his skin seemed more darkly tanned than ever, emphasising the startling brilliance of his eyes.

'Well?' he prompted her. 'I haven't changed all that much in ten days.'

'Yes, you have. Your tan has deepened.'

'The sun takes care of that.' The mocking eyes gazed into hers. 'I hear Peter is home for the weekend?'

'Now where would you hear that?' she almost wailed. 'Have you got spies behind every bush?'

'No more than I need. Let's go up to the house, I must say hello to your mother and Patricia.'

'That's very civilised of you. They'll like that.'

Julia and Patricia were more than delighted, they were thrilled.

'It's strange, but I thought we'd see you this weekend,' Patricia told him softly, her expression dreamy and rather fey.

'Look, why don't I take you for a ride?'
Relaxedly Thorn Sinclair disposed of his coffee
cup—their very best.

'Oh, heavens, Thorn!' Patricia was like a little
child. 'I'd be too scared!'

'You'll get a wonderful bird's eye view of the
entire valley, and its really quite safe.'

'Go along, darling,' Julia said sweetly. 'I'm sure
Thorn will look after you.'

'There's room for you too, Susan,' he said.

'Well, *I'm* sitting beside you!' Patricia clasped
his arm.

From the air the valley was a dream, a
complete novelty in both girls' lives, and Susan
felt the fierce love of it rage through her. She
saw again the long, coiling ribbon of the creek,
the silvery lagoons, the rounded, rolling undula-
ting hill, the tree-lined ravines and in the
distance the majestic ranges. Today they were
pure larkspur, their outlines sharply distinguish-
able in the pure air.

They came down on the old McKenzie property,
once a fine station, soon to become a multi-
million-dollar sporting resort.

'Oh, my legs are wobbly!' Patricia wailed and
clung to Thorn's arm. 'I've never seen the valley
like that before.'

Susan walked away from them both, trying to
relate the complex plan she had seen to this well-
known landscape. The old homestead looked
terribly run down and slightly forbidding, even
haunted. How perfect if dear old Miss McKenzie
were to walk about frightening the golfers! And
yet Miss McKenzie had never seen the place as
going on forever. The property had been left to her
great-nephew, Alistair, which would have turned
him quickly into a fairly wealthy man. There was

even a shade of Miss McKenzie sitting out on the ramshackle verandah which was rather disquieting. Sunlight outside, deep shadows within.

'Feeling all right?' It was Thorn.

'I was looking for Miss McKenzie, but she's not there.'

'Perhaps it's too hot for you in the sun?'

'Funny!' Susan retorted sarcastically.

'We're going to make all this so Miss McKenzie will approve,' he told her. 'Certainly her heir was very enthusiastic.'

Susan shook her head. 'Because he never knew the valley.'

'When is the project starting?' Patricia asked him appealingly. 'It's already quite a topic of conversation in the town, Geoff was telling me. Most people are all for it.'

They tramped all over the place, with Thorn outlining his plans for the great course. 'Of course, nowadays given the money and the technical knowhow, it's possible to build a golf course just about anywhere, but this particular valley is really nature's gift. It has everything to make it great—the setting, the natural hazards, the precise contours of the land. Donald Scott, the architect, thinks we can get together a championship course, and he's designed all over the world.'

'You play yourself, of course, Thorn?' Patricia looked up at him with admiring eyes.

'Not as much as I used to. Making one's fortune seems to play havoc with freedom, but I'm going to change all that. I've worked almost twenty-four hours a day for the last ten years, and now suddenly I want to leave it to somebody else. I don't think I'd be going too far to say I'd like to stay in this valley forever.'

'You mean retire?' Patricia looked dismayed.

'Not exactly. I can't ever see myself retiring, but I can sure change my way of life.'

'Just don't try to move too fast!' Susan warned him with glint in her green eyes.

They lingered for at least another half hour, and almost despite herself Susan became interested and absorbed. She was even, she noticed to her chagrin, the only one who was asking him at all relevant questions. Patricia was picking her way through the emerald, wildflower-strewn grass as though the sight of her was enough to burn itself in a man's memory. She wasn't really following the conversation at all. But that was Patricia if, for some reason, things didn't interest her.

When they returned, they were greeted by Peter and Elizabeth, who came out on to the verandah, flashing smiles.

'Wouldn't I like a trip in that!' Peter exclaimed.

'You would?'

'Oh, yes! It would be a great way to see the property.'

'Then please, be my guests.' Thorn Sinclair included Elizabeth in his smiling charm.

'I felt nervous up there,' Patricia later admitted to Susan, 'did you?'

'Not at all. I was too busy checking out what passed below us. It must be a great way to muster cattle. No wonder they used helicopters on the big properties.'

Of course he stayed to an early lunch and it was a taste of joy because he kept them all laughing. Even Julia was heard to gurgle, a sound that was quickly cut off when Thorn let it be known he had asked Susan out to dinner.

'Well that would have been lovely, Thorn,' she

said with gracious firmness, 'but of course Peter is home.'

'Actually, Mamma, Elizabeth and I were going into town to see a movie. "Arthur." They tell me it's very good.'

'A movie?' gasped Julia.

'You don't mind?' Peter flashed her a white smile, aware of the softening effect it had on his mother. 'We never get to see anything the way it is.'

'But *I'm* not doing anything,' said Patricia.

'Then come with us.' Peter put his arm around her graceful shoulders and hugged her. 'Susan deserves a break.'

'I hardly think Thorn asked you himself,' Julia later challenged her younger daughter.

'He did too.' Susan started to pull her entire wardrobe out on to the bed. 'Paddy isn't the only one who can go swanning it. I'm entitled to a night out too, Mamma.'

'I've never really understood you, Susan,' Julia sighed. 'Obviously Thorn is being kind, but I don't think I'll ever forgive you if you ruin things for Patricia.'

'Remember I'm your daughter too, Mamma.' Susan turned hurt, beseeching eyes on her mother. 'I know Thorn Sinclair is a highly eligible bachelor, but right at this moment he belongs to nobody—or if you want to put it another way, he belongs to us all. Paddy has had first pick of everything ever since I can remember.'

'She *is* older than you are, after all.'

'Of course she is!' Susan was starting to feel very frayed, 'but surely that doesn't mean I'm forever to step aside?'

Julia compressed her finely cut mouth. 'I will not have you ruining things for your sister! Hers is a gentle temperament. You rather force yourself on people. Your manner is far too challenging.'

'Thank goodness! Susan said very clearly. 'Now, I don't like to be rude, Mamma, but I have to dress very quickly. Paddy might find it a transfiguring experience to give Annie a hand tonight—always supposing she knows where the kitchen is.'

'The more one appeals to you, Susan, the more perverse you become. Have your evening out, by all means, but do try to act prudently. I well remember how you botched Patricia's romance with Brett Casey.'

'Heavens, Mamma,' Susan lamented, 'am I ever going to throw that off? Brett Casey made a pass at *me*. It was *me*—or I, if you like—he found strangely desirable. I'm a wronged, wronged girl.'

Julia looked unconvinced, unforgiving, and walked to the door. 'You're lucky your sister is so forgiving,' she snapped.

'Or at any rate in blinkers. I don't know why you try to turn her off Geoff, Mamma. They happen to be the same kind of people.'

'And you're Thorn Sinclair's kind, I suppose?' Julia stared back at her daughter, unsmiling.

'Please don't get upset about this, Mamma. Can't I have a night out? If Thorn is really interested in Paddy I'm no threat to her. There's nothing wrong in accepting his invitation, yet you're making me feel as if I'm doing something dreadful.'

'Some people, Susan,' said Julia, leaving, 'make waves.'

It was a test to even begin to get dressed. Susan collapsed on the bed wondering if she was doomed to be forever eclipsed by her sister in her mother's eyes. So many maternal feelings surged in Julia's breast, for Peter, the only son she adored, for

Patricia, the image of Julia's youth, but clearly Susan was regarded as a changeling, almost somebody else's child.

'Woe is me!' she cried aloud. Why was she carrying the burden of so many worries? Why didn't she just sell up and get out? Losing Cobalt Downs wouldn't be the end of the world. She spoilt it all by giving a loud wail of distress.

'What are you wearing?' Patricia came in with drowned eyes.

'Oh, Paddy, you haven't been crying, I hope?' Why had she ever accepted this dinner date? Too many cards were stacked against her.

'I saw him first!' muttered Patricia.

'You did *not*!' You're altogether too forgetful, Paddy.'

'If you want to go. *Go!*' Patricia snapped. 'Don't mind me.'

'Boy, you and Mamma know how to attack!' Susan felt a little tearful herself. 'All *I* know how to do is slave my guts out while you and Mamma sit up on the verandah drinking tea, and I don't even rate a Saturday night out!'

'Not with *my* man!' insisted Patricia.

'He's not your man, Paddy. Don't be absurd. He's being nice to us both for his own reasons. It just so happens I'm as attracted to him as you are, and he's rich enough to afford marrying us both.'

'I can't possibly go with Peter and Elizabeth,' Patricia protested.

'Why not ring up your old chum?'

'He's in Sydney for the weekend,' Patricia volunteered the information. 'His aunt died and left him some money.'

'Isn't that always the way!' sighed Susan. 'When people have got a lot someone dies and leaves them some more. You'd better watch it. Geoff is at that stage in his life when he wants to get married. If *you* don't have him, some other girl might be delighted to.'

'He's too staid—too dull.'

'And he worships you like an angel. You like worship, Paddy. Ever thought of that?'

Patricia actually bowed her golden blonde head and cried, and the tenderhearted Susan, for all her quick tongue, rushed to her.

'Look, Paddy, if it means so much to you, I'll stay home. Heck, what's a bit of excitement! I knew before I started it I should abandon.'

Patricia turned off the tears with incredible speed. 'But he'll be here in thirty minutes!'

'Say I've gone to hospital to have an operation. Say you're better looking and much better company. Say what you like.'

And now Peter knocked on his sister's door. 'Susy, is Patricia in there?'

'What does he want?' Patricia looked around blankly.

Peter looked around the door with raised eyebrows. 'Where did you get to, Paddy? Are you allergic to housework or something?'

'Not allergic, Peter. I have a positive horror of it.'

'It's the sort of thing girls do,' said Peter. 'Elizabeth is giving Annie a hand at the moment.'

'Are you reproaching me?' Patricia asked.

'Not at all. Why don't we both clear out and leave Susy to dress?'

'She shouldn't be going out anywhere,' Patricia wailed. 'Mummy's in a fury.'

'*What!*' A grimace of violent distaste crossed Peter's handsome face. 'I just can't stand this any more! You and Mother are forever ganging up on Susan. You're a beautiful girl, Paddy, but Susan is very compelling. I think Sinclair's interested in her and so does Elizabeth.'

'And you know all this from a brief visit?' Patricia asked scathingly. 'Thorn is interested in me!'

'Then why did he ask Susan out?'

'Because he's kind.'

'Your judgment, sweetie, not mine. When are you ever going to be honest with yourself?' When is Mother ever going to allow you to be?'

'Clearly,' said Susan, 'I'm not going anywhere.' She didn't even bother to look at her watch.

'Don't be crazy, Susan.' Peter pulled her up off the bed. 'You're a free agent and so is Sinclair. I heard him say he'll be here at seven, so you haven't got much time to get dressed.'

'It's like some sort of plot between the two of you!' Patricia wailed.

'Calm down, Paddy, and grow up. You don't have to think what Mother thinks. Think for yourself.'

'You're a pig, Peter!' Patricia raised her head and mopped her eyes. 'You needn't think I'm going along with you and Elizabeth to play gooseberry.'

'Yes, you are. I know you're going to love Dudley Moore—all the girls do.' Peter took hold of Patricia with one hand and opened the door wider with the other. 'Enjoy yourself, Susy. It'd be nice to see you all dressed up, but we'll have to leave if we want to catch the first feature.' He gave Susan a conspiratorial wink.

'Do you think I could borrow your white silk dress, Paddy?' Susan called.

'No, you can't.' Patricia sounded very tearful again. 'And if you dare wear it, Mummy will tell me.'

'Oh, Paddy,' Peter said sternly, 'you're a real Christian! Wear your green, Susan. You might have had it a while, but that doesn't mean a lot. It looks terrific on you.'

'You've always sided with Susan,' Patricia accused him.

'Because she's the gutsy one,' Peter returned unflatteringly, 'and that's that!'

CHAPTER SEVEN

'YOU'RE very quiet.'

The sound of his voice cut off Susan's upsetting thoughts. 'I'm sorry, I was miles away.'

'You mean you were back home.' Smoothly he accelerated and passed a dilatory car. 'Why didn't you put me off if you can't live with the thought of crossing your mother?'

'Is it that obvious?' She glanced up at him, suddenly very tired of all the domestic problems.

'Obvious all round. Extraordinary as it may seem, your mother acts as though she only has one daughter.'

'Don't please criticise Mamma to me,' said Susan coldly.

'But she tried to stop you, Susan. Didn't she?'

'She wants the best for Patricia.'

'And I'm the best?' he asked drily.

'Yes.' Susan was more than usually blunt. 'It's really your fault, you know. If you aren't really interested in Paddy, you should never have encouraged her. She takes things very much to heart.'

'Come, little one,' he glanced at her, 'how did I encourage Patricia?'

'Oh, Thorn, I don't know. You've certainly tried to perturb me.'

'Because we strike sparks off one another, you see. Patricia is absolutely delightful, but if I may be so ungallant, I have nothing to apologise about. In spite of what she thinks, or your mother thinks, I assure you my manner has been no more than casually friendly. I haven't, for instance, kissed her or thrown her in a pond.'

'But you must have said *something*.' Susan gave his rugged profile a measuring look.

'Nothing I can remember.'

'No wonder, you're such a fast worker!'

'Stop lecturing me, Susan,' said Thorn as though he had had enough. 'I'm long past playing corny little games. If you want honesty, you'll get it. I've enjoyed women in good measure—a few of them a lot more dazzling than your sister and accomplished to boot. Patricia is very young. She has a lot to learn. I have absolutely no interest in her, sexual or otherwise. On the other hand, I'm not sure about you. You're very young too. It bothers me.'

'The extent of my experience?'

'Exactly.' He managed a brief laugh. 'As a rule I avoid involvement with innocent young girls.'

'You find experienced women more exciting?'

'I want to make love to *you*.' The velvety, vibrant tone roughened.

'*Oh!*' Abruptly her whole body began to shake.

'See what I mean?' He gave her a dangerous, slanted glance. 'Why would I want to get involved with a frightened teenager?'

'I'm twenty.'

'Twenty!' He gave an exasperated laugh. 'Try to understand what the hell kind of mess this could be.'

'Then let's turn around and go h-h-home,' she stammered, ashamed of her weakness.

'You don't want to go home, Susan, damn you!'

'Why are you so angry?' She turned to him with a little gesture of desperation.

'Actually I was perfectly all right when I arrived, but then I began to see how awkward everything could be. The last thing I want is to make your life any harder.'

'So okay,' she said in a fierce little whisper. '*I* won't fall in love with you, Mr Sinclair. Neither will I let you take advantage of me either.'

'Good for you, Susy!' he said with an amused indulgence she didn't understand. 'You haven't even asked me where we're going.'

She could have said, who cares, as long as I'm with you, instead she said crisply: 'As long as we're not leaving the country, I don't mind.'

'I thought you might want to see my penthouse at the Coast.'

'You're joking!' She was trying to take in the enormity of it, deciding he was only taunting her.

'We'll see.'

She was tingling from the toes up. 'I've never tried to hide the fact that I'm a good, old-fashioned girl.'

'Just as well.'

'Now what does *that* mean?' Perversely the hard possessiveness of his tone jarred her nerves. 'It's very convenient, isn't it, a man's attitude? He can do anything he likes, but the woman he's interested in must keep herself exclusively for him.'

'Don't complain,' he said drily. 'It works.'

Susan didn't remember much of the trip after that, except that it was fast and incredibly smooth, and soon they were in the centre of the Gold Coast's dazzling lights.

'Where *are* we going?' she wavered. There were many excellent restaurants. Which one? Across a table was close enough, her pulses were thrumming.

'My penthouse—I told you.' The left indicator came on. 'It's right on the beachfront, the new Golden Sands. It's one of my enterprises, along with three partners.'

'But surely you're not going to ask me to cook dinner?'

'One of these days I'll try you out, Susy, but I've engaged caterers for tonight.'

For a few frantic moments she toyed with the idea of jumping out, but his attraction for her was getting so powerful excitement was overriding caution. It would be so easy to let him have everything he wanted. So easy ... when she wanted so much herself.

In the lift Thorn took her hand and she couldn't speak. She would have given anything to be more sophisticated and sure of herself, but she felt in her bones that despite his worldliness and obvious sexuality he would be a man she could trust. Thorn Sinclair wouldn't need to force a woman, but it still made him very dangerous, all the same.

'You needn't hold my hand so tightly,' she said as they made their way along the thickly carpeted corridor.

'In case you change your mind.'

'My mother thinks we're dining out.'

'Too cool on the balcony. Don't forget we're thirty floors up.'

'It's frightening how rich you are,' she said. 'I always thought Grandpa was the richest man in the world.'

'Instead he only lived like it!' Amusement lines etched the sides of his mouth. 'He was a very flamboyant personality, your grandfather. I suppose that's where you get a lot of your dash from.'

'Oh, I say!' He had opened the door to his apartment and the sight of it made her voice go jerky. 'It must be nice for a summer vacation.'

'Is it anything else *but* summer at the Gold Coast?'

'You know what I mean.' She wandered past him, staring around her. A large painting and a bronze sculpture marked the entrance hall, both reflected in a mirrored wall. The bronze, a reclining woman, looked like Henry Moore and Susan turned to Thorn with a very wide-eyed: '*Is* it?'

'Yes. I bought it about five years ago in London.'

'Good evening, sir . . . madam.' A white-coated, black-trousered caterer introduced himself with considerable panache. 'Everything is ready when you are. Would you care for a drink now?'

Thorn chose champagne for them while Susan continued her circuit of the large living-dining areas of the penthouse apartment. A sweeping expanse of glass looked out over the glorious, rolling Pacific Ocean, a superb panorama by day, but at night the interior of the apartment commanded all the attention.

It was the most polished, tailored luxury she had ever seen—a crisp, male elegance, which was not to say a woman couldn't fall in love with the whole thing. The gleaming timber flooring was set in a herringbone pattern over which magnificent Heriz rugs made a rich statement. The seating was lavish to the point of opulence, all a pristine white with cushions for lively colour. There were more paintings and sculptures, floating in the glowing white, open spaces, luxuriant plants in fabulous brass pots, and along one wall the most beautiful six-panelled Chinese screen Susan had yet seen, although there were several of high quality at home.

'This is gorgeous,' she said, and touched a reverent finger to a translucent jade panel.

'The concubines of the Emperor Chia Ch'ing. Rather fetching, aren't they?'

'*I'll* say! And eight for the one person.'

'Didn't Solomon have two hundred wives, and no one thought the less of him.'

'It must be difficult to actually keep to one.'

'Depends upon the person.' Thorn glanced down at her gleaming head. 'The other side is very beautiful as well—birds, animals, flowers. You have some fine screens at the house.'

'Mm. Grandpa bought them. He would have loved this. Early nineteenth century, isn't it?'

'You're very knowledgeable, Susan,' he commented.

'Grandpa and I used to go off to galleries all the time. He was a compulsive buyer, you know.'

'A collector in the heroic mould. You actually have a small fortune in the homestead.'

'And I'm not parting with it either!' She turned to him swiftly, her green eyes enormous and sparkling. 'Grandpa meant his buys to stay in the family. Wherever we go we'll all get our share and and I hope we'll pass our pieces on to our families.'

'Then you're definitely in the marriage market?'

'Certainly. But not for some time.'

The waiter delivered their drinks unobtrusively and withdrew.

'Lovely.' Susan sipped very slowly at hers. The champagne bottle in a silver bucket now stood on a silver tray atop a white-brass mounted Korean chest. 'Do you entertain here often?'

'A lot over the Christmas–New Year. Businessmen are always entertaining, Susan. It goes with the scene.'

'*Women*, I mean.'

'A few. Do you mind?'

'Fortunately, no.' She looked down into her wine flute, her thick black lashes masking her eyes. 'Please don't think you have to show me the bedroom.'

'The master bedroom, you mean?'

'You may well smile.' She raised her glass a little recklessly.

'I was merely wondering if you were imagining mirrors embedded in every wall.'

'Of course not.' Now she looked flustered.

'In any case, newcomers are generally never invited,' he assured her.

'That takes a lot of character, not to speak of co-operation,' Susan observed.

'You're suggesting, of course, that you would never co-operate?'

'Why don't we change the subject?' She gave him a reproachful look. 'We seem to be running into a lot of trouble.'

They did not eat at the streamlined dining setting, a sparkling hexagonal table with a bronze glass top surrounded by Oriental-style chairs, but at an intimate setting for two, a circular table softened by a beautiful cloth that fell to the floor; drawn up to the night-time view of a purple sky crowded with stars. One of the heavy glass doors had been opened a few feet and she could hear the ceaseless gentle roar of the surf, smell the moist, beautiful salt air. It was infinitely arousing, far more so than atmospheric music, though in fact she now realised soft music was carrying through the apartment, light classical music with the violin being played by a master. Menuhin, she considered. It had just his exquisite, singing tone.

'You're going to spoil me,' she said, after Thorn had seated her.

'I want to.'

After serving with their first course, fresh New Zealand asparagus, cooked to perfection and served with some delicious buttery sauce, the caterers became invisible, reappearing as if by magic to serve the second course, a chicken and rice dish that even managed to look Spanish and had been, in fact, prepared by a Spanish chef.

'This is delicious!' said Susan with quick appreciation. 'On the scale of one to ten, I'll give the chef eleven.'

'I'll pass it on.' Thorn was watching her with considerable indulgence, apparently amused by her healthy appetite. 'Do you know how many women I've invited to dinner who just taste everything, then put their knife and fork down?'

'Semi-starvation is not my style,' she assured him.

'I can see that.'

'You said you wanted me to be happy.'

'I do.' He looked at her with something like tenderness. An expression that rendered Susan almost speechless. Thorn Sinclair, *tender*? It must have been a trick of the light. There were no conventional light fittings to speak of, but an almost totally concealed array of downlights that illuminated required areas in the most fascinating and functional way possible. It also meant no one would have to clean thousands of droplets on chandeliers, a task she and Annie found increasingly insupportable.

'I think you have the most beautiful apartment in the world,' she said dreamily.

'You haven't seen all of it. Once the dessert is served the caterers can leave. We can fix ourselves up with the coffee.'

'Oh!' Her voice sounded almost shaken.

Dessert was a beautifully decorated chocolate mousse with the subtle orange flavour of Cointreau, and now they were on their own.

'Any more and I'll go to sleep!' Susan sighed.

'Good black coffee will wake you up.'

'No liqueur.' She watched him open a squat bottle.

'All right. I considered a liqueur might be too strong for you anyway, and the last thing I want is to have you tipsy.'

She touched the delicate spray of orchids that blossomed from a Japanese pottery bowl and served as a centrepiece. 'This has been like magic for me,' she told him.

'What about a walk along the beach?' Thorn suggested.

'Perfect.' In any case, now they were alone too much excitement was building. A brisk walk with the tang of the sea in her face might sober her up, or at least provide a breathing space.

'Stop looking at your watch,' he said, his face changing, hardening just a little.

'I can't be *too* late,' she explained.

'Why not?'

'Never mind. I'm sure you have a good idea.'

'You'll be twenty-one in April.'

'How do you know?' She looked back at him in surprise, her green eyes with the emerald sheen of her very best chiffon dress. It was more than two years old, but it was dateless, tiny bodice, fitted waist, a lovely floating skirt. It clung to her slender body in all the right places and showed just the suggestion of the shadowed cleft between her small, perfect breasts.

Thorn took his time to answer, his examination of her leisurely but curiously intent. 'I didn't have to use any of my powers of persuasion on Annie. She told me everything about you, from the moment you gave your first hearty squawl.'

'Annie loves me, but she is inclined to go on,' said Susan apologetically.

'Actually, I found you a most fascinating subject.'

'Back to your lazy drawl?' She met his mocking gaze with a direct one of her own.

'Finish your coffee, little one, and we'll go for a walk.'

'Besides, it's a good deal safer!' Now why had she said that? It was what she had been thinking, but did she really need to blurt it out?

Fortunately Thorn didn't appear to hear.

Several minutes later they were strolling along

the beach with the outgoing tide sighing melodiously, a ravishing breeze blowing and a sky full of shooting stars.

'Isn't this the most wonderful way to relax?' Susan decided to skip away from him, enjoying the crunch of gleaming sand through her bare toes. Little gusts of sea breeze were whipping through her hair, lifting her floating skirt so it whirled around her body.

'Don't get too far ahead of me, Susan,' he said. 'I want you safe.'

She had to remember it was the beach at night, very magical, but still not the safest place for a lone nymph. She walked back to him and took his hand. 'I'm learning new things about you all the time. You're very protective, aren't you?'

'Especially when you clutch my hand like a little girl.'

'Oh, but it's too dangerous to be a woman.'

'I know.' He was joking with her, but very lightly.

'I really love the ocean, don't you?'

'Yes. It takes all my tension away. Even you have forgotten yours.'

'Thank you for a lovely evening, Thorn.' She turned her head up to look at him, her gilded skin turned to pearl.

'I guess you're going to tell me you have to go. Isn't that it, Cinderella?'

'It really is a long way back.'

'In a Ferrari?' he said in a calm, matter-of-fact way. 'I think if you're in by one, it will be all right.'

'Listen to the breakers against the rocks!' Suddenly she was over-excited and panicky.

'We'd better be going back.' He still held her hand, his dark voice low-pitched.

'All right. Where you lead, I follow.'

They found her sandals where she had hidden

them in a crevice, then they walked quite naturally arm in arm back to the floodlit tall building. Susan had thought a brisk walk would bring her tumultuous feelings under control, but she could feel her whole body flushed with heat.

In the lift she put a hand to her tousled hair, talking too much to cover her nervousness.

'Relax, Susan,' Thorn said. 'Seduction is out of the question.'

'Good. I couldn't handle it.' She shook her head a little, as though dazed. 'I couldn't possibly, Thorn.' Why not? Because she knew he could tear her heart out? Her nervousness and confusion showed itself in the abnormal brilliance of her eyes. 'What do you say we should wash up?'

'Susan, please!' He spoke calmly, though his eyes too were jewel-like in their intensity. 'Come and sit down.'

'Okay——' She turned away with a little laugh, focusing upon a single armchair.

'Not there—here.' He caught her hand and swung her to him like a dancer.

But then as she looked up at him it was like the same electric jolt shocked their bodies. She was unable to stop moving into his arms and they closed around her powerfully, enfolding her lily-slim body.

'Kiss me, Thorn,' she said, without the slightest tremor, compelled.

'Kiss you?' he muttered, as though he wanted something very different, but as she sighed, he lowered his head and cut off her breath.

She wasn't ready for passion, was she, but it was rushing for her. Gathering her up like a king-tide. Her eyelids fell heavily over her eyes and he slid his hands up and down over her back, moulding her to him, causing an ardent sexuality to flower within her. She was learning so quickly, exploring his mouth as he was exploring hers, her small hands trying to get to his skin. She couldn't pretend. She was crazy for him.

'*Susan,*' he murmured. Not clear at all, but very deep and drugged.

Now was the time to draw back, to stiffen, but she couldn't. This was too splendid, unknown. A fantasy with flashing lights.

Thorn lifted her as lightly as though she was a feather, seeing the high flush on her cheekbones, her features made more beautiful by intensity. If she opened her green eyes, they would be huge, the green of deep waves crashing against rocks.

'Open your eyes, Susan, and I'll stop.'

'I don't want to.' her voice was small, rather husky, very far away.

'You're a child.'

'No!'

'I must protect you. Even from me.'

She knew better, twining her arms like clinging tendrils around his neck. 'You want me—I *know* you do.'

'Why you of all people!' His hand slid down over her breast, a caress so intimate she jerked her head back in ecstasy.

'Damn, damn, *damn!*' He sounded as though he hated both of them, but his hands had a life of their own. Now both of them cupped her breasts and they were half sitting, half lying together on the deep sofa with silk cushions piled at her back.

Susan didn't even want to think about her own sensuality, but she wanted his hands on her bare flesh, not on closely draped chiffon. Thorn must have known it too, because he drew in his breath sharply and as she stirred and arched her back unzipped the tiny bodice and peeled it away, frowning almost angrily as he lifted her dress away and threw it away so it landed draped in a fragile drift across a chair.

She was half naked now except for briefs and an ivory, lace-edged half-slip, her only defences against her own longings. She heard him let out his breath at the sight of her body, and she was fiercely glad that it was beautiful and so exquisitely fashioned to respond.

His lips brushed her nipples, then closed over one with hard urgency, and she gave herself up to sensation she had never known, liquid mercury flooding her body.

'My little Susan, you're beautiful!' He lifted his head, his hands still enclosing the lovely symmetry of her breasts.

'You're beautiful too. I didn't know a man could be so beautiful. You're so powerful. I love the smell and the taste of you. It's terrible, really, to feel so wild!'

It was an admission that incited him, petrol heaped upon flame. The touch of his hands on her body was more voluptuous than anything even remotely within her experience and she began to utter tiny, inarticulate moans, sounds of pleasure so shattering it bordered on pain.

'Help me, Susan,' he muttered, his voice ragged. He took his mouth from hers and his hand from her heart-shaped body.

'I *can't*. I want you so.' She was drenched in rapture, thrusting her body still closer to his. If hell-fire was about to consume her, she didn't care.

'Taking you would be terribly wrong. You're so young, so lovely. And there's another reason— you're a virgin, and you don't love me.'

'Oh Thorn, I don't love you and I feel like this?'

She opened her beautiful eyes and they were full of tears.

'Susan, don't cry.' Now he cradled her like a child.

'You've broken my heart,' she whispered.

'Never.' He traced exquisitely gentle fingers across the marks of her tears. 'You tie me up in knots, do you know that?'

'It doesn't seem like it,' Susan said pathetically. 'I'm afraid of you.'

'Don't be silly.' She touched a finger to the deep cleft in his chin. 'You're the strongest man in the world. Anyone can see that.'

'Am I? Heaven help me!' It was said very tensely. 'If you were only a few years older, we wouldn't be talking now.'

'What chance have I of becoming a woman if you won't love me!' She even hit him along the hard wall of his chest. 'I'm not a frivolous, promiscuous girl. I feel deeply.'

'And yet you don't know exactly how you feel about me.'

She tossed her head away, but Thorn held a hand beneath her jaw and turned it back. 'Well?'

'You excite me in every way possible.'

'And that's about the size of it—infatuation.'

Susan thought for a moment, her emerald eyes wide, the lashes long and spiky with tears. 'No, much more. Probably I'm bound to suffer for it. Can you tell me what you feel about *me*?'

'Perfectly, only it's rather more important to establish *your* true feelings. I'm years older than you. On my own admission I've lived a full life. I know what I want. You don't.'

'Do you want me?'

'*Yes!*' There was a little antagonism mixed up with the stress.

'For good, or just for a little while?'

Thorn shrugged his wide shoulders. 'You'd only die if I took you away.'

'Heaven knows why you think that. Peter said I was like a rare plant, but what I feel for you right now is swamping what I feel for Cobalt Downs.'

'So you'll sell it to me?'

'Ah!' Hard, cold reality flooded back. She touched her feet to the carpet, then stood up, as perfect as a figurine. 'I daresay you might do anything to get what you want.'

'Gently, Susan, gently,' he cautioned. 'All I want right now is to pull myself together. In any case, I should have known what to expect.'

All the way home Susan was very quiet and distant, withdrawn into her own disturbing thoughts. How easy it had been for him to put her under his spell, but what deep motives underlay it? It was horrible, grotesque, to think he was using her; yet at the same time his own feelings were highly complex. He could have taken her, almost without effort, but he hadn't. He had been the one who had taken a strong grip on his heavily taxed control.

'Don't think ludicrously foolish thoughts, Susan,' he told her quietly as they pulled up a little to the side of the house.

'Goodnight, Thorn.' She threw open the door and hurried away, but he was alongside her in seconds, pulling her into his arms.

'Now do you believe me when I tell you you're too young?'

'I may be young,' she said bitterly, 'but I'm smart.'

'And that makes me a villain, I suppose? I'll do anything to get your property?'

'*Yes!*' She flung it at him with her head thrown back in challenge.

'You nasty little brat!'

'No, I told you I'm *smart*.'

'How can you be when you talk like an idiot?
Oh, go inside, for Pete's sake. This has really been
a terrible strain.'

'You devil!' She drew back from him in outrage,
then discovered that wasn't enough. How dared he
make her love him, *hate* him—destroy her. Rage
flared in her, humiliation. She brought up her
hand and despite every carefully nurtured instinct
hit him sharply across the side of his arrogant face.

He grasped her wrist and nearly spun her off her
feet. 'I really cannot imagine what I see in you. Stop
tearing into me, you little savage, and run inside.'

'You're a fine one to talk about savages!' she
cried, but then the terrible lump in her throat
stopped her. She fled from him out of the star-
studded night and into the longed-for privacy of
her room, where she lay face down on the bed and
cried out her unutterable misery. Of all the serious
things she could have done, she had to fall in love
with a shocking manipulator! It didn't seem
possible Thorn was such a fool as to tell her, but
then he too had been far from himself. What she
really should do to have her revenge on him was
charm him out of his mind. Play the part of Anne
Boleyn shamefully without ever losing her head.

When she finally stood up, her face was very
white and her eyes swollen from crying but
resolute all the same. She staggered through to the
bathroom to wash her face and clean her teeth. How
unspeakable to go to bed with make-up on. Even in
the midst of calamity her training came through.

'I'll show him!' she said aloud, and stared at
herself fixedly. 'I'll bring him to his knees!'

Nothing like a big man to fall hard and far.

She would have slept in very deeply, but Patricia
was avid to hear what had happened.

'Wake up, Susan. Come on, it's after seven.'

'Wh ... a ... a ... at?'

'I said, wake up!'

'Oh no, not an interrogation?' Susan rolled over on to her back and looked rather blearily into her sister's determined face.

'What happened? Mummy and I waited up until after twelve.'

'How was the movie?' queried Susan.

'Terribly funny. You should have seen it. Where did Thorn take you?'

'Oh, Surfers,' she said offhandedly. 'It takes such an age to get there and back.' In fact, time had flown.

'So what else?' Patricia shook her. 'What did he do? What did he say?'

'He was absolutely delightful. A most pleasant companion.'

'Oh, heavens!' Patricia gasped. 'Tell the truth.'

'He ravished me. Absolutely *inspired*!'

'Mummy will get it out of you,' Patricia said crossly. 'She certainly thinks you should have declined the invitation.'

'But I didn't care to.' Susan sat up. 'I do hope you and Mamma understand. After all, loyalty can be taken too far.'

'Why, you're in love with him!' Patricia sank back, blinking her blue eyes rapidly.

'In love with him? Thank you, no. I'm somewhat smitten, but not entirely burned.'

'Oh, how dreadful!' Patricia straightened up, her fingers to her lips. 'How beastly you are, Susan. You enjoy taking my boy-friends off me.'

'*Boy*-friends?' Susan gave an unamused hoot of laughter. 'He's no boy—he's a hawk!'

'If you ruin this for me, Susan, that will be the last straw!' Patricia threatened.

'*Paddy!*' Susan's laughter died quickly away. 'Be serious now. Thorn Sinclair isn't in love with you. He thinks you're absolutely delightful. He may even have teased you and passed admiring remarks, but he's a very experienced, sophisticated man. He's actually passing admiring remarks to women all the time, but it doesn't mean anything.'

'He's my property!' Patricia said convulsively.

'Rubbish!'

'We'll see what Mummy has to say about that!'

Susan looked away, out of the french doors, and shrugged wryly. 'It's high time, Paddy, you began to think for yourself. Mamma has managed to convince you that every man you meet falls for you on sight, and maybe they do, partly. You're certainly very lovely, but don't waste your time or your tears on Thorn Sinclair. He's much too cool for the likes of us.'

'You know you're trying to take him off me!' Patricia fumed.

'On my word as your loving sister, I would never break up a relationship where one existed. I don't doubt Mamma has encouraged you, but I do assure you he regards both of us as very young. Very young, get it? As in profoundly easy to bowl over. Actually I've planned a small surprise for him,' Susan added.

Patricia's rather placid expression lit up with anger. 'You're a schemer, Susan, and you're jealous because I always put you in the shade.'

'You don't you know,' Susan said quietly, waving that charge aside. 'All through my teens I was downright popular. At the risk of offending you, some people actually like black hair and green eyes.'

'Oh, Susan!' Patricia sighed, torn between a very real sisterly love and what she had been fed on all through the years. 'He's such a wonderful prize. I've been waiting all my life for such a fabulous man.'

'Would it break your heart if I landed him?' Susan asked.

'Mummy won't let you!' Patricia staggered back in shock. 'What are you talking about, Susan? You're quite mad when you get going.'

'No doubt!' Susan muttered. Perhaps there was some truth in it. 'But we have to find some way to hold on to Cobalt Downs.'

At that, Patricia caught herself up, spun around and raced back along the gallery in search of her mother's counsel. Where Cobalt Downs was concerned, Susan was capable of anything. Wherever could Mummy be?

Susan knew what the response would be.

'Please tell me, Susan, what you have on your mind,' Julia later asked wearily.

'Nothing much, Mamma.' Susan wiped her soapy hands with a tea-towel.

Are we to wish you luck with Mr Sinclair?' Julia asked ironically.

'Mummy!' Patricia cried, somewhat nonplussed.

'To spare your ears, darling,' Julia said tenderly, 'why don't you go outside?'

'I'd rather stay here.'

'*Please* go, darling.' Julia said impressively, and Patricia went.

'Now what is this Patricia is babbling on about?' Julia asked.

'In a way,' Susan began, a little nervously, 'I think Thorn Sinclair quite likes me.'

'Precisely. Beauty is not quite adequate.'

'Now what does that mean?' Susan asked in amazement.

Julia gave her younger daughter a long, thoughtful gaze. 'It distresses me to have to say it, but even *I* think you are more interesting than Paddy.'

'You haven't helped. Mamma, telling her everyone is in love with her.'

'Haven't you noticed that for a beautiful girl, Patricia is quite without confidence?' Julia asked gently. 'She's as innocent now, as much an Alice in Wonderland as the day she was born. Surely you can understand that. You were never to think I didn't love you, Susan, as much as I love Patricia. The difference is, you didn't need me. Your character, too, emerged very early. You were always independent and energetic, the apple of your father's eye. I used to despair that he was trying to turn you into a boy, but he always used to say someone had to be responsible after he was gone. I think he always knew he would die comparatively early. And there's the other thing. You're so much like him.' Julia's face puckered into an expression of despair. 'Every time I look at you, I think of what I've lost. I loved him so much.'

'Oh, Mamma!' Such rarely admitted agony was too much for Susan. She went to her mother and hugged her. 'It's not my doing I look so much like Daddy, it's *yours*.'

Julia pulled herself together and uttered a soft: 'Goodness! If I've leaned towards Patricia and Peter it's because I know they haven't got your strength. In any case, you're entirely different from me. I came here to Cobalt Downs because it *is* beautiful and I loved your father so much I would have followed him anywhere. Now he's gone, nothing is the same. I've always hankered after the sophisticated life, not a rural existence, yet I married a man who was wedded to the land. Poor Patricia is just like me. There's no question she needs my help.'

'But she's really very fond of Geoff,' Susan

pointed out sagely. 'He understands her and worships her, and though she occasionally calls him very dull and staid, she gets very angry if anyone else attempts to do the same. Another thing, she's not in the least interested in domestic details and Geoff will have the money to afford a housekeeper. She would *have* to marry someone with money. She hasn't had the slightest possible training for roughing it.'

'Yet it seems as if you might be the one to marry money?' Into Julia's eyes came a speculative gleam.

'The signs are there,' Susan agreed, 'at a price. And the price is Cobalt Downs.'

'Be more explicit, Susan,' Julia said sharply.

'Would you wish him luck, Mamma?' Susan asked.

'For Pete's sake!' Julia stared at her daughter in utter amazement. 'Do you mean he wants to buy it, when he already owns half the valley?'

'The McKenzie half is business. He would, if he could, live on our half. Lord of the Valley. He's already told me his plans. He wants to bring Cobalt Downs back to what it was, and he's especially capable of it. He's rich, clever, vigorous and extremely determined. He's also just discovered he's sufficiently attracted to me to endure marriage and remove my grip on the land.'

'This is unbelievable!' Julia sank into a chair. 'Make me a cup of tea, please, Susan. What on earth did Annie go off for?'

'Shopping. It's absolutely necessary, Mamma.' Susan filled the electric kettle and plugged it in.

'Count on you for something extraordinary,' Julia sighed. 'Has he actually *said* he wants to marry you?'

'Marriage may be of the essence. He won't get Cobalt Downs otherwise.'

'And how do you feel about him?' Julia lifted

her head and watched the colour rise in her
daughter's face. 'Why, my dear child, you're in
love with him! So soon?'

'I'm not in love with him. I loathe him!'

'Hardly likely, if you can colour like that. Also
he's an intensely attractive man. If he wanted to
move a woman, he could.'

At that moment Patricia ran back into the
kitchen, almost weeping with frustration. 'What's
going on?' she demanded.

'Sit down, darling,' said Julia, 'and have a cup
of tea.'

'But I hate tea, Mummy.'

'I'll make us a cup of coffee,' Susan said.

While Susan was managing both, Julia explained
the situation to Patricia while Patricia wrestled
with acceptance.

'I don't believe this!' she said, echoing her
mother.

Julia put a hand on either side of Patricia's
lovely face and kissed her. 'Believe it, dear.'

'But what's going to happen to *me*?' Patricia
shuddered. 'I drove Geoff wild when I told him I
was in love with someone else. He could be
rushing about wildly trying to find a new girl.'

'Would you care?' Susan set the creamed coffee
down before her sister.

'Of course I'd care!' Patricia looked indignant.
'Geoff belongs to me. It's just never occurred to
him to look at anyone else.'

'But surely—if you told him you were in love
with someone else?'

'Yes, I did. He said he'd shoot himself.'

'Well, he hasn't yet. Julia blinked rather rapidly.
'Frankly, I didn't think he had it in him.'

'He's really quite passionate,' Patricia told them,
'when he gets worked up.'

'Good for him!' said Susan, and gave a peal of laughter. 'Why don't you drink your coffee, then ring him. He's adored you for so long—but men do strange things when they're hurt.'

'Yes.' Patricia smiled tenderly. 'I don't think Thorn would ever be faithful. He's too attractive.'

A terrible coldness enveloped Susan. That could be a possibility.

When Peter and Elizabeth came in from their leisurely inspection of the property, they had had a slight disagreement.

'Elizabeth thinks you have far too much on your hands,' Peter turned on his sister a contrite face. 'She thinks I should be doing more—and she's right. There've been plenty of weekends I could have got away, but I stayed in town. There was always Elizabeth. I wanted to be with her, and I knew she and Mother wouldn't hit it off.'

'Give them a chance, Peter,' Susan begged. 'Don't go putting the idea into Elizabeth's head that Mamma doesn't approve of her.'

'Well, she doesn't, does she?' Peter sniffed.

'Give her a little time to come round. Elizabeth is a sensible girl.'

'My dearest love!'

'Aren't you lucky, Peter?' Susan smiled at him, thinking that was indeed so.

'Why can't Mother see what *I* see?' he sighed. 'Of course, I'm in the doghouse a bit. I told Elizabeth she rather conceals her looks a bit. She does, you know. She had to dress up for a mutual friend's wedding once, and you would scarcely have known her with her hair all done up and a bit of make-up on. She's got a lovely figure too.'

'I agree.' Susan looked at her brother with a touch of sympathy. 'Perhaps she may make a little more effort when she realises it pleases you.'

'Well, it does and it doesn't. I don't really care. It's people like Mother who really care. I just said maybe she could dress herself up more when she comes.'

'So that's why she rushed up to her room?'

'The last thing I ever want to do is hurt her,' said Peter earnestly. 'But you know families. Try to keep everyone happy and you'll lose your mind.'

Elizabeth obviously wasn't one for the sulks, because a few minutes later she was downstairs again, smiling at Peter radiantly, her long straight hair braided in the latest fashion. She had changed her blouse as well for a form-fitting T-shirt, but as she had beautiful, high breasts Peter launched himself at her and kissed her.

'I've got to make a phone call,' said Susan, 'but why don't we give Elizabeth a riding lesson? She's got to learn how to ride.'

'Do you think I'll be able?' Elizabeth turned a hopeful face to Susan.

'Of course. We'll show you.'

In the privacy of the study, Susan dialled the penthouse apartment's number. At first it rang and rang, then as she decided he obviously wasn't there, and why should he be, she answered.

'Sinclair.'

'Thorn?' Susan injected a breathless, pleading little note into her voice.

'Yes. It couldn't be Susan.'

'It is.' She clutched at a drawer with a little burst of excitement and it slid out and spilled the contents on to the floor. 'Damn!' she muttered.

'What's up now?' He sounded hard and amused.

'Please, Thorn,' she was back to the little-girl voice, 'I wanted to apologise for last night. What I implied was unforgivable.'

'You can stop the cajoling, you little monster. It doesn't ring true.'

'It *is* true!' She was fighting to stay in part.

'Forgive me,' said Thorn, 'but you're wild enough to do anything. What are you on about now? Bringing me to my knees?'

'What's that music?' she asked suddenly. Background sounds were growing louder, one of Billy Joel's songs and the sudden clamour of voices.

'I have a few people here,' he explained.

'Dammit, darling, do come! Business, business, business, even on a Sunday!'

There—she heard it, as clear as a bell. A woman's voice, confident and laughing.

'You have to go,' she said hurriedly.

'No, I have a minute.'

A sob was starting up in her somewhere. Oh, she must have been out of her mind to imagine Thorn Sinclair was seriously interested in her! It was the property, of course, and his private life aside.

Keeping cool and controlled was a desperate struggle. 'Well, I won't detain you if you have friends. I just want you to know—*You'll Never Get Cobalt Downs!*'

So there it was, disaster, and her control was woeful. She crashed the phone down and kicked the drawer with her foot. The beastly creature! Patricia was right. How could any woman expect a man like that to be faithful?—not that he had any reason to be faithful to her. It was just so humiliating, that was all. Probably he could make love ardently to a different woman every night. He had a decidedly sexual aura, a challenging look in his silver eyes. Moreover, he was a bachelor and perfectly free to indulge in any philandering activities he liked.

She almost sobbed aloud in black despair. Damned rotten men! They were all delinquent.

Wives, mistresses, blended in for good measure. No one could call a man *darling* like that, unless she knew him pretty intimately. It had sounded so utterly sophisticated, the voice of a confident and experienced woman. Hadn't Thorn said himself he had enjoyed women in good measure?

How disgusting! she thought furiously. How disgusting to try to seduce me with herself doing everything possible to help him. How appalling that this was the way things were. In an attractive man's hands, a woman was putty. It was one of the truly alarming facts of nature.

It was no use moping, and she couldn't allow herself the luxury. There was Elizabeth to be entertained and the crowd of people along the creek. They expected to see her, have her point out the best picnic spots, that kind of thing.

For the rest of the day she wore herself out, and if she expected a return phone call, one wasn't forthcoming. The best thing she could do was lick her wounds and recover. The most shattering experience of her life—which only went to prove how little experience she really had. Only women were decent, faithful, dependable, but when their feelings were involved they did really stupid things. Temporary blindness to reality. Well, she was clear-eyed now.

CHAPTER EIGHT

ONE only had to listen to catch the sounds of activity on the other side of the valley. Work on the exclusive Cobalt Valley resort had begun and in the adjacent town people stood about having earnest discussions on what the resort might do for their part of the world.

'It should be terrific!' Geoff enthused, coming to seek out his beloved at the earliest opportunity. 'Always fancied the game myself.'

Susan had shaken her head and muttered something, but Patricia had looked at her long-time swain of hidden fires and smiled, the same smile reflecting no trace of a misguided infatuation gone wrong.

'What are ya tryin' to do, girlie?' Spider asked Susan after she had come back from exercising Mephisto. 'Ya were cuttin' it fine with that fence.'

'Don't worry, Spider,' she assured him. 'He's a superb animal.'

But Spider took off his hat and scratched his head. 'I can't 'elp thinkin' Mr Sinclair is right. That 'orse is too strong for the likes o'you.'

'Don't I always bring us safely home?' Susan challenged her old friend.

'Reckon ya do, but I thought ya'd go flyin' that time.'

Annie, too, was concerned. 'What's wrong, me darlin', please tell me.'

'Nothing wrong, Annie.' Susan tried to maintain her aplomb.

'Oh yes, there is. I know you too well.' Annie

171

looked up from her mixing bowl to study the girl shrewdly. 'What's happened to Mr Sinclair? I was sure we'd be seeing him soon.'

'I expect he's far too busy tearing up the valley.'

'Now, love!' Annie shook her head chidingly. 'Mr Sinclair appreciates beauty. He won't have any flash resort. It will be just like he said— nothing ugly or commercial. The beauty and tranquillity of the valley won't be spoiled. As well as that, love, it's creating jobs and bringing more prosperity to the town. Norm, the butcher, was telling me the tradespeople expect to see a big rise in profits. Workmen and their families will be billeted, and besides, the people will get to share all the benefits. The young people are especially pleased. And the polo should be exciting. Peter was even talking about getting up a team. He may not be grazier material, but he sure is a good horseman.'

'Mamma was nicer to Elizabeth, wasn't she?' Susan admitted.

'Mamma is being nicer to everyone,' Annie seconded with gratitude. 'I wonder if being here without your father was getting her down. She hasn't had a break, you know, not since. . . .'

'No.' Susan bowed her head. 'There doesn't seem any real way, Annie, that I can contrive to keep Cobalt Downs. I had a dream, but the reality of it is I can't afford it. I'm not considering Mamma. I think of myself as a loving daughter, yet I'm trying to do something in the face of my family, and although they're against it they've really gone along with me—for Daddy. But Daddy's not here.'

'We're doing much better,' Annie felt compelled to say, saddened by these first signs of defeat.

'Thorn Sinclair's doing. He's interfering here,

there and everywhere. I should have known Rick didn't turn up right out of the blue. He was sent here—by Thorn Sinclair, master of intrigue.'

'I think you love him,' Annie said shrewdly.

'How can you love someone you don't respect?'

Annie tried to see what was behind the haunted look in the large green eyes. 'And why don't you respect him, love? He seems to me the kind of man to command that kind of thing effortlessly.'

'He's a philanderer,' Susan said bitterly.

'Now there's an old-fashioned word!' Despite herself, Annie laughed.

'Well, how else can I say it?' Susan flushed a bit in embarrassment. 'Lady-killer, wolf, the Sheik of Araby?'

'Doesn't sound like any of those things,' Annie's manner clearly implied that she didn't agree with Susan's crushing estimation.

'I've never known anyone who could make me feel so completely vulnerable.'

'I expect that's because you've never been in love. Lovers *are* very vulnerable.'

'He doesn't love me, Annie,' Susan said. 'I wish I could punch him in his haughty nose. I expect that's how it got broken in the first place.'

'I like it,' said Annie. 'He'd be just too handsome without that hump in his nose. Why don't you ride over to the other side of the valley and see if he's about?'

'Never!' Susan exclaimed wrathfully, and her green eyes flashed fire. 'Thorn Sinclair is the last man I'd chase after. He's a hypocrite!'

Annie looked up with a very puzzled expression. 'Whatever did he do to you?'

'Do to me?' Agitation seized Susan. 'He made me love him, that's what. And it's not fun at all, it's horrible!'

'Now, now, don't fly into a temper. Why don't you try to talk it out?' Annie checked the girl quickly by grasping her arm.

'There's nothing *to* talk about, Annie,' Susan sobered abruptly. 'Except maybe what I've tried to avoid all my life. Selling Cobalt Downs.'

Eventually her own desperate feelings drove Susan back to the old McKenzie property, and at first it seemed her worst fears were confirmed. Workmen swarmed everywhere, on foot and in heavy machinery, and extensive clearing and levelling operations had already begun on the beautiful, rolling terrain. There were even huge deposits of sand, she assumed for the bunkers, gleaming like pyramids in the noon sun.

The old McKenzie homestead had been levelled and concrete poured over the greatly enlarged site; the clubhouse, as she recalled. Miss McKenzie would never have sold had she not been old and an invalid. Susan hoarded her unhappiness to her, refusing to see what this giant enterprise might become. Now it was wrecking the calm of the valley, a threat to its tranquillity and peace.

She stood on the small hillock and held back the branches of a golden acacia so she could look down, unnoticed, on the teemingly busy scene. Two men were standing in the middle of a new clearing, both of their heads poring over plans. Neither of them was especially tall, and Susan's small face twisted in a pained expression. She never wanted to see Thorn Sinclair again in her life, now she was upset because she didn't see him. Only the experts, the workmen he employed.

'Well, well, *well*!' a voice said behind her softly. 'How odd that you should hide yourself up here, Susan!'

Her mouth was dry and she touched her tongue to her top lip. 'Think of the devil!'

Something deep in his eyes went very still. 'You look as if you've been unhappy.'

'Who, *me*?' Haughtily she tilted her chin. 'I'm much too busy to be unhappy, Mr Sinclair.' His eyes were still fixed on her and she turned away angrily. 'You're making an awful mess of the valley.'

'One gathers you're not familiar with projects in their early stages, so I'll forgive your appalling ignorance.'

'Oh, dear, have I offended you?' she murmured.

'Not really.' His half-smile was silken and faintly threatening. 'I'm quite willing to show you over the place, if you want to see.'

'How gracious of you, but I'm afraid I haven't got the time. Tell me, have you bionic vision or something?'

He ignored her derision but took a step closer. 'One of the workmen reported a flashing silver light up here. It's the sun on your rear vision.'

'Oh.' Susan glanced over to the parked jeep. 'Surely that wasn't worth an inspection?'

'I must be psychic,' drawled Thorn. 'I suspected it would be you.'

'I can't accept that.' She stared at him, raising her delicate winged brows.

'Nevertheless it's true!' He seemed as engrossed in her as she, unwillingly, was in him. 'What are you so bitter about?'

'I told you—I'm not bitter about anything, except perhaps this.' She turned and indicated operations with her hand.

'It's got nothing to do with you, Susan,' he pointed out.

'No, it hasn't.' The sight of him was unbearable

to her—his silver glance striking her face, the arrogance that lay on him like a patina of light. 'I expect you're busy, so I'll say goodbye.'

'Why did you hang up on me?' he asked briefly.

'I must have felt like it.'

'You started off so sweetly, then ended up in character.'

'Well, you know how it is with young women,' she shrugged. 'They get over-emotional.'

'About what?'

'Take your hand off my arm,' she said rigidly, realising he was angry beneath the smooth exterior.

'I'm amazed I don't put you over my knee!' snapped Thorn.

'And that is one reason why I can't abide you. You're just the type of man I despise.'

'Nonsense!' His eyes narrowed to slits and now he grasped her fine-boned shoulders. 'The fact is, Susan, you care about me more than you want to.'

'You're terribly conceited, aren't you?' she said recklessly. 'I find men who have always got to prove their power over women pathetic.'

'How have you gone so long without a psychiatrist?'

'Let me go,' she said furiously, 'before I lose my temper!'

'Oh, for pity's sake, don't do that! Look at you, a spitting little cat—and about what?'

'I hate you! You're bruising me!' She turned up her face to meet his glittering eyes.

'I'm still waiting for you to explain.'

'What a great pity, because I'm not explaining anything. Let me go, you *oaf*!'

Thorn looked down at her wildly flushed face, his formidable face set in lines of hard anger. 'What an offensive little brat you are. Sadly, since you have no parent to do it, I'm going to give you the paddling you so richly deserve.'

'Try it!' She had never looked more mutinous or more near hysteria. 'You great big bully, stay exactly where you are!'

'Susan, Susan,' he clicked his tongue as though she was beyond saving but it was his clear duty to try. 'I'm sure you'll be grateful to me in the years to come.'

She was lifted willy-nilly and carried over the grass to a fallen log, where he swept her over his knee and administered several hard slaps to her small, shapely rear. 'Spare the rod and spoil the child, but it's over now!'

This isn't happening, she thought dazedly. It *isn't*. There are rules about this kind of thing. She tumbled off his knee feeling faint. There were no tears to fight. She was so shattered about what kind of man he was—brutal, tender, passionate. There was little doubt he had some mental disorder.

'You can get up,' he said coolly. 'You know quite well I haven't hurt you, merely taught you a lesson.'

Still she lay there, too bemused to get up. Besides, she was so very tired and the smell of the grass and the rich earth was comforting. It was curious really the way she was feeling, melting, detached, a small part of her smarting but the rest curiously serene. People fainted at the oddest times, maybe she was fainting now.

'*Susan?*' Suddenly Thorn sounded appalled at what he had done. 'Susan!'

He was down beside her, turning her gently so she lay on her back. Her slender body was dappled with sunlight, her lips parted, but her eyes closed.

'I'm perfectly sure you're all right.' His hands touched her forehead, her face.

'Then why do you sound worried?' It wasn't an accusation, just a question.

'Extraordinary,' he said tersely, 'a minute ago I wanted to beat every inch of you.'

'And now?' She opened her green eyes and they were enormous, her golden skin impregnated with colour.

'I only want to make love to you, treat you like something precious.' He put out his hand and ran it over her breast as though he was unable to stop himself. 'Imagine—all the women I've known, and it had to be you.'

She gave a deep, fluttery sigh. 'I bet you've never known anyone you treated like me. If I told anyone it would be a scandal. Women are liberated, you know.'

'Really?' he sounded surprised. 'You're not even tame.'

'How dare you hit me,' she said.

'Do you really hate me?'

'My word, yes!' She turned her face so he couldn't look into her eyes.

'Because I hurt you.'

'You didn't hurt me.' She tried to press her face into the wonderfully clean scent of the grass.

'Are you afraid to look at me or something?'

Into the curious serenity came the old, familiar erotic excitement. She could even feel the tips of her breasts tingling. 'That's about it, Mr Sinclair. As I think I mentioned very early in our acquaintance, you're a dangerous man.'

'You're just as dangerous to me.' He slid an arm under her and lifted her into his arms.

The urge to respond to him became irresistible, but she knew that pain always followed this intense pleasure. She couldn't tell him that she had overheard that woman at his penthouse. The very day after he had made love to her with such passion and—protectiveness, yes. That would be betraying herself too much. Letting him know the agony he had inflicted. In resistance lay her pride and security.

She pushed away from him with her hands, but he caught them and buried them against his chest. 'What game are we playing now?'

'Damn it, we both know who plays games!' she cried with sudden passion. 'I wonder what your girl-friend would say if she could see us now?'

'Girl-friend?' His eyes gleamed like silver coins.

'You told me yourself you had plenty.'

'I've never said "I love you," not once.'

'You wouldn't!' she said bitterly. 'You're not husband material at all. You're a wicked, devilishly attractive man.'

'And rich. Don't forget rich. You wouldn't be interested in me if I were poor.'

'Of course I wouldn't!' she lied fiercely. 'A poor man could never save Cobalt Downs.'

'And you'll suffer a fate worse than death to save it?' His eyes speared across her in a searing glance.

'What have you got in mind?' She was determined to play this game, but her head hurt.

'You and me.' The harshness of his expression gave him a faintly satanic look. 'Would you marry me, Susan, in return for a half share of a restored Cobalt Downs?'

'Is that the best deal you can offer?' she said stubbornly.

'Well, you're not getting the lot. I wouldn't trust you, little one, not to attempt to throw me off.'

'This is a business deal, is it?' she asked in a voice so brittle it could have broken.

'People do make business deals. Even men and

women. I'll buy the property for a fair price. We'll set up your mother and Patricia in an appropriate manner wherever they want to go, then we'll settle down to connubial bliss.'

'I want a contract,' Susan said. 'Partners, but no connubial bliss. I may not love you, but I would fight and sulk and screech if you maintained a mistress on the side.'

'Well, why would I want a mistress?' Thorn asked drily, 'I'd have you.'

'I don't know,' she said, quite unable to keep to the spirit of the thing. 'I think I'd be ill, marrying without love.'

'And you're sure I couldn't get you to love me?'

'I suspect you'd try.' Suddenly her lashes were wet.

'Don't cry,' he said curtly. 'I don't think I could stand that.'

She gave a strange little laugh. 'Are you the only one to make people suffer?'

'Because I didn't ring you. Come to see you?' His hand closed under her chin.

'Because you're dishonest.'

'How?' His hand tightened on her throat.

'If it makes you feel any better, choke me.'

'Oh, you're ridiculous!' he exclaimed violently. 'The only way I'm going to get any sense out of you is get you in a double bed. But failing that . . .'

It started out with violence on his part and a lack of surrender on hers, but then their combined chemistry became so powerful, profound, it destroyed all considerations of the mind. Susan ceased all her struggles, although he was holding her so fiercely even her slender bones were imprinted against his and gave herself up to his mouth and his hands.

'You love me, you *know* it!' he muttered.

'No.'

'Yes,' he answered, his voice hard and imperious, matching the dark severity of his face. 'I want you—I want you, even though I'd like to strangle you.'

But now she looked utterly defenceless and young and he muttered something beneath his breath and bent over her again.

'Marry me.'

It was impossible to fight out of this, wildly flowering, heated world, but she tried.

'Keep still.'

She was beyond even the slightest of struggles.

'Do you know you're the most maddening girl in the world?'

'I . . . I . . . .'

'But I still want to marry you, and that's one of the reasons I'll save your precious Cobalt Downs for you. If you ever look sideways at another man or attempt to refuse me I shall beat you. Got it?'

She stared upwards into his blazing eyes. 'I won't let you own me.' The duality of men! *She* would never be allowed to look at another man. *He* could do as he pleased.

'Then tell me why your body cries out to be owned?'

'Because . . . because . . . I want you too.' It was difficult to deny it when even now his hands were still on her breasts with a sensitivity more undermining than violence.

'Then I think we'd better get married, don't you? I want you in my bed as soon as possible. In fact, I can't imagine what's stopping me now.'

'Maybe it's because I'm fainting away.'

'You wouldn't, if you'd eat something,' he said. 'I can count all your ribs . . . like this. . . .'

Susan let out her breath slowly, then flung up

her arm and drew his dark head down to hers. 'I don't love you, you know. I'm merely crazy about you.'

'A bit, yes.' He grasped a handful of thick, silky curls, then closed his mouth over hers.

So it was decided, but at the very mention of wedding bells, the normally sedate Patricia suffered some kind of brainstorm when she insisted with overflowing eyes that she should be the first to go.

'I'm the elder daughter. It's traditional I should be the first to marry.'

'Well, just arrange it, my darling!' Julia viewed her unexpectedly angry child. 'What a lucky man Geoff is, to be sure.'

'Don't expect to top, Paddy,' Peter told Susan, when he heard. 'The thing is, once Thorn buys the property, we can all afford to get married. Even me. Who knows why Elizabeth and I should wait. We might have had to once, but now everything is different.'

Except that this isn't going to be a proper marriage for me, Susan thought. She always kept hearing that female voice, but never once did she mention it. If she did, she might betray her flaming jealousy, and it was impossible to be jealous without embracing love. Neither of them mentioned the very word. It was a marriage of convenience, with white-hot passion thrown in.

At least it had been, but now Thorn acted in a strangely companionable manner. He kissed her quickly when he arrived and when he left, both times usually in full view of everyone. He never once took her hand or drew her aside or hustled her into some room where they could be alone. Nothing was any fun. He didn't even react to all her

banter, so eventually she fell silent, presuming
that the very thought of marriage had sobered him
abruptly. He didn't even look at her with anything
even vaguely approaching lust, though she had
bought a lot of new clothes. Maybe he had lost his
passion for her. She couldn't tell.

Four weeks later, Patricia and Geoff were
married, very worshipfully and romantically,
Patricia, in her wedding finery, so exquisitely what
a bride should be that there was scarcely a dry eye
in Cobalt Downs superbly manicured home
gardens. Susan and Elizabeth served as attendants,
their mid-to-dark brunette colouring and their
lovely rose and sea-grass long, sheer dresses
adding definition to Patricia's bridal white and
gold.

'I'm so happy, *happy*!' Patricia breathed,
clinging to her new husband and fighting for
composure. 'I'd have loved to be home for the
wedding, Susan, but we'll be away for months.'

Julia had cried continuously, more the old-
fashioned watering pot than anyone who ever
knew her could credit.

'My baby! My precious girl!' She looked
resplendent in an elegant silk ensemble, while a
long-time family friend, now a widower, comforted
her gruffly and clasped her hand.

By the time it was all over, Susan was
exhausted. She was even frightened. She felt like
running away. Patricia and Geoff weren't exactly
highly-strung, hyper-rapturous lovers, but they
cared deeply for each other; they were well suited
and demonstrably compatible, so what had *she*
done?

'Darling, you'll have to stop rushing around.
You look so glowing, you're electric.' Thorn
caught her whirling figure with one hand, but as

he looked down at her with lazy amusement, he saw that her eyes were full of tears.

'*Susan!*' he exclaimed.

She looked up at him uncertainly, a wild rose flush staining her cheekbones, her emerald eyes flashing not fire but some kind of poignant message. Why did he have to call her 'darling' like that? He could have said it in a brittle, mocking way, but no he had to say it so her heart turned over. Her mouth started to tremble and she knew without question that she was no match for him at all.

His dark-timbred voice seemed to deepen with tenderness and a quick concern. 'When you look at me like that, we just *have* to get lost.' He lifted his head and looked out over the crowd. 'Ah, there's Julia, with that Whittaker fellow in tow. I'll just have a word with her. You sit there and don't attempt to move.'

'Yes, Thorn.' He was too strong for her, too managing. Out on the terrace Peter and Elizabeth were dancing, Peter's hand making little convulsive movements on Elizabeth's back. No doubt Peter and Elizabeth were in love. Everything they did together had a great sureness. Elizabeth had decided to match herself to her future in-laws. These days her easy elegance was drawing eyes. Of course Susan understood why she had made the effort. She loved Peter and she knew she had to win the approval of his mother. Hadn't Julia introduced her all around with the light of pride in her blue eyes? Yes, Elizabeth had passed the test, but Elizabeth was a clever girl.

Thorn came back to her at last and lifted her with two hands at her narrow waist. 'Come away, little one. We've done our duty, now we're on our own.'

'But where are we going?' she asked, in a strained breathless voice.

'I want to be alone,' he countered gravely, 'don't you?'

They spoke to Peter and Elizabeth on the way out, Elizabeth saying something teasing, then they were in the car and away into the night.

'Were we really supposed to leave?' she asked, bewildered, turning her head so she could see his strong profile.

'I'd say so,' he said tersely. 'Why don't you tip your head back and relax? This last week has been very tiring for you.'

'We're not going to the penthouse, are we, Thorn?' She gave a little cry.

'You think I'm going to make love to you in a *car*?'

'I wish you wouldn't. Please!'

'You wish I would.' He shook his dark head. 'I'll take very good care of you—of that you can be sure.'

To avoid any more disturbing conversation she shut her eyes and the smooth flight of the car lulled her. He was more necessary to her every day. Necessary for survival. She would gladly have exchanged her beloved Cobalt Downs for a life on the other side of the world with him. In its way, this kind of love was terrible, not a mutal fondness, a deep pleasure in one another's company, but a raging flame. It was consuming all her old ideas. She believed she couldn't go another day without mentioning how deeply anxious and disturbed she was about that woman's voice, the sound of which had driven deep into her subconscious. She had even tried repeatedly to say that 'darling' with the same languorous, throaty tone, a kind of sophisticated yearning, but it always came out rather clipped and businesslike instead. Where was her self-respect? She couldn't possibly marry a man who had one standard for her and another for himself. Though it was done, and it bit very much into the female psyche.

Her considerations wore her out and when she finally came out of it she was moaning.

'Susan, what's the matter?'

It was obvious they had arrived, for they were parked in the basement and Thorn was gripping her by the shoulder.

'Goodness, I must have dozed off.' She sat up apologetically.

'I've never heard anything more piteous than those little moans. Let's hope you weren't dreaming about me.'

'Never. Look how conceited you are already!'

He glanced at her drily. 'You must be feeling better. What a pity! I was enjoying those tears in your beautiful, troubled eyes.'

'You're not so rich that you can make me happy, Thorn,' she said.

'Don't be absurd. You won't allow yourself to be happy, for some reason. And that reason I'm going to find out if I have to lock you in a room!'

In the lift Susan looked down at her pretty gold sandals and her toenails. They were painted shell-pink—the first time she had ever painted her toenails in her life. She had pretty feet. Small and narrow, only without Thorn, she wouldn't be able to buy shoes.

In the apartment she had difficulty coming away from the mirrored wall.

'If you want to admire yourself, go ahead.' Thorn came up behind her, tall and stunningly good-looking in his dress clothes. 'In my opinion, you left everyone else in the shade.'

'Patricia looked like a lily.'

'Certainly she did, but they're not everyone's favourite flower. I like something a little more *dynamic*-like a satiny Oriental scarlet poppy that bursts out of bud.'

'My dress is nice, isn't it? Thank you for advancing that money.'

'Thank you for accepting it,' he reponded drily, his brilliant eyes rather heavy-lidded. 'You're just beginning to look cherished.'

There were strange, leaping lights in his eyes, and as Susan swayed, he drew her back hard against him, his arms locked around her beneath her breasts so they were facing their twin reflections.

Beside him she looked very small and almost impossibly fragile, her bare shoulders gleaming, the sea-green of her lovely filmy dress like blossom against the sombre cloth of his suit. Now his hands shifted to cup her breasts and she made a curious little sound.

'What's worrying you, little one?' he asked quietly. 'Why are you fighting yourself and me?'

Susan was trembling, but she covered his hands with her own. 'I think I've just discovered I can't pretend marriage. It was a beautiful ceremony today. It *meant* something.'

'In short, you don't think our marriage lines would?' A dark, brooding expression moved over his face.

'Why do you really want to marry me, Thorn?' she cried tragically, and spun around in his arms. 'Please tell me. I must know. *Now!*'

'So you can do what? Wield even more power with that tiny hand?' There was an edge to his voice now, and she closed her eyes for a moment.

'I have no power over you.'

'I could eat you.'

She was aware of her whole body trembling, of a wild roar in her ears, then simultaneously Thorn coiled her body up into his arms and his mouth covered her open lips.

They lay together on his bed with the moonlight streaming in through the great expanse of glass and soft lamps lit on either side of the bed. They had reached their limits of love play, and now Thorn was finding his own driving urges were becoming too powerful for them to stay where they were, though temptation was dazzling.

It was somewhat different for Susan. She had totally surrendered, realising she had reached a point where she could deny him nothing, because what she felt for him was unmistakable—an eternity of love.

'You seem afraid to take me?' Her voice was as soft as the breeze.

'You can say that again!' He turned his head to regard her with faint self-mockery. 'What if I should make you pregnant? I don't want you pregnant so soon. I want you all to myself for a good year at least. And memory is long, Susan. On your wedding day I want you to come to me as a bride. I want it especially because it's what *you'll* want. I know I'm taking you too far, but with you, it's like the tide. I keep getting pulled under even though I think I'm strong.'

'You *are* strong,' she said.

'Oh, really, am I?' He groaned and stood up, pulling on his shirt. The light glistened on his black hair, his bronze skin and the almost pure silver brilliance of his eyes.

'I love you,' she said, and let her head fall against her raised arm.

'Why, Susan!' He turned sharply and his very glance was an act of ownership.

'I think I like to say it. *I love you.*' Now she turned over dreamily on her back, the light playing over the delicate contours of her body.

'And when did you discover it—now?'

'No, I think when you called me Sonny.'

'Then why all these senseless games?' He caught her fragile wrists, pinioning her to the bed.

'You shouldn't have to ask.'

'I *am* asking, Susan.'

So then it tumbled out, what she wanted, expected, thought she might be getting.

Thorn got up and moved off as though he was extremely annoyed. 'You mean you thought I was having an affair?'

'All the time.' She sat up her eyes as green as a lorelei's.

'Because you overheard a woman's voice on the phone?'

'*Twice.* Once in your office. Once here.'

'And you've been keeping it to yourself all the time?'

'I'm just a stupid kid,' she muttered.

'So help me, you are.' He came back to her, bent over the bed and kissed her hard on the mouth. 'I imagine the voice you heard was Karen's. Karen Varney.'

'The actress?'

'I know Karen very well,' he told her. 'She used to be madly in love with me when we were both about twelve years old.'

'One wonders when she stopped?'

'Jealous?' he glinted at her.

'Well, why not? She sounded incredibly sexy and she looks pretty good too on television.'

'We'll invite her to the wedding. We'll invite

Noel as well. That's her husband—Noel Varney, the producer.'

'And he lets his wife speak to you like that?'

'He can't help it. That's her voice and everyone is darling in the theatre.'

'How dull we must all seem by comparison,' Susan said drily.

'If you want to know,' Thorn sat down and leaned towards her, 'you're the only woman who's ever entered my bloodstream. I want you in every way possible, physical, mental, emotional, love and friendship. I love you and I determined on you right from the beginning as my wife. Still, I pushed it aside for a while. She's only a kid, better face it.'

'So what happens now?' Her voice dropped to a husky entreaty.

'I'm going to get you dressed and home. It's a matter of honour.' He put one arm behind her and held her to him. 'Can you picture our wedding day, Susan? Can you *now*?'

For a moment the situation was precarious, her radiant face haloed in light, then she saw what was in store for them and allowed him to pull her up. One night soon they would be together in just the way that they wanted. Their wedding night with a sky full of jewels.

Harlequin® Plus

A WORD ABOUT THE AUTHOR

Born in Brisbane, Australia, where she lives now, Margaret Way cultivates a varied life-style that suits her vivacious personality to a T. She says, "I'm a creature who feels exaltation at heights"—referring to her love of her hilltop home—though she could also mean her zest of life, which she lives to the fullest.

With her teenage son, Lawrence, and other family members, she especially enjoys tearing off to the beach every weekend. Haunting galleries and auctions is another of their hobbies. They generally come home with more than they can afford because they find paintings, sculptures, porcelain and pottery too tempting to resist.

Margaret loves children and music, and she is an excellent cook and wine authority. She especially appreciates French champagne on weekends and on "every possible joyous occasion." There's one thing she doesn't like, however. "I am not and never have been given to long walks," she comments, "preferring to drive my Jaguar, which I madly enjoy, and why not? It's a great way to travel!"

As for romance, Margaret was once married but today prefers the single life. She says of her characters, "My own heroes are the only ones who can make me respond with alacrity."